The Celebrant

A story about the people we don't see.

by

Chris Parker

Chiselbury

Published by Chiselbury Publishing, a division of Woodstock Leasor Limited
14 Devonia Road, London N1 8JH

www.chiselbury.com

ISBN: 978-1-916556-08-9

A Casual Glance

'So many people offer the world nothing more than a casual glance,
they see only a glimmer of all that is around and within them.
Based on that
they create their beliefs,
make their decisions,
shape their lives;
with only a glimmer to inform them
they convince the next generation of the truths
that must be upheld
in order to justify their own existence.'

Epiah Khan

'I have no idea!'

Bella.

The Ending

i

'Death doesn't ask for permission.

'Death chooses when to reach out and lead us away, leaving loved ones behind, creating a previously unknown space and silence.

'Yet despite the inevitability of death, despite the way it tries to fill the landscape of our mind and make us think of nothing else, death is also – and far more importantly – a reminder of that which precedes and surpasses it.

'And that which precedes and surpasses death, that which surrounds it with the shining light of opportunity and experience, is the most important thing of all: life itself.

'It is because of life, the all-encompassing, ever-enduring nature of life, that we are ultimately here today.

'We are here to remember, and celebrate, the fact that life, not death, is the greatest of all powers. Life is the greatest gift. It is through life that we share our dreams, our hopes, our beliefs and, of course, most importantly, our love. It is through the sharing of our love that we create those moments, those memories, those eternal connections, that death can never touch.

'It is through the sharing of our love that we create friendships and family, those invincible, invisible forces that are as powerful as the very air we breathe.

'Anne-Marie Rose Fairbank created and shared such love. She lived such a life. And we, who shared that love with her, are here today to celebrate her life and to show our gratitude for the many positive ways she influenced us all.

'Of course, at this time, you might be asking yourself the questions, "How can I possibly celebrate in the face of grief? How can I possibly be grateful for my loss?" And there, again, love is our salvation.

'Every breath can be a reminder of the enduring power of love. With every inbreath we can learn to feel Anne-Marie's presence just a little more clearly. With every outbreath we can let go of our grief just a little more easily...'

There are one hundred chairs in front of me. Ninety of the chairs are empty. Ten people are sitting in the front row, close to the pulpit behind which I'm standing.

Anne-Marie's Shade is standing next to her coffin. She hasn't moved since I first arrived. She hasn't tried to communicate with me. I've respected her silence and offered only a slight nod of my head and a brief smile. I believe she will see everything she needs to in my eyes.

I continue with my speech. It's written on A4 sheets of paper, in capital letters, in Times New Roman, font size 18. The sheets are in a simple, black plastic folder. It fits perfectly on the pulpit. People can see me turn the pages, but they never see the actual folder as I do so. I'm pretending that I need to keep glancing down, to remind myself of what I'm going to say next. The truth is, I memorised it days ago. I just don't want any of the ten people to know that.

I'm sure Anne-Marie's Shade worked it out before I began.

She is standing still, straight, serene.

I turn another page in my file. I glance at it just long enough for everyone to notice. I'm coming to the end now.

'So, as we prepare to leave here now, we can make a commitment, a promise to remind ourselves every day that love is a verb – it's a doing thing, shared between people.

'No matter where those people might be.'

I look deliberately, briefly, at each person sat in front of me. Then I close my file. It's a physical metaphor. Another

3

small ending. I always do it like this. People need to be readied to leave. Actually, most of them want to go. They just don't want to acknowledge the fact. It helps if I'm the one telling them to move on.

Which is what I'm about to do.

In this crematorium, each funeral must be in and out within thirty minutes. Mourners leave out of the south-facing doors, so they don't see the next lot gathering outside the north-facing entrance. Time management is the second most important part of my job.

I step from behind the pulpit.

As I do so, Anne-Marie's Shade smiles at me and points at something I can't see. Her smile broadens. She waves, takes three steps to her right and disappears.

I cry spontaneously.

It's not my most professional move.

ii

Let me tell you the most important fact:
> *Death starts before it starts and ends after it ends.*

That's worth spending some time over.

In fact, and you should trust me on this, it's worth spending some time over right now.

iii

You didn't, did you?

You just ignored me and rushed on.

You treated the most important fact like it was a headline, rather than an invitation to question and explore. You treated it like a headline because that's what we've become conditioned to do. Just accepting the headline means we don't have to do any work. We don't have to consider what we don't know. We can just choose the headlines that support those things we are sure of. And we can ignore the rest.

Can't say that I blame you.

We live in a know-it-all, no-time-to-waste, keep-your-eyes-on-your-phone, produce-your-own-podcast, I've-got-all-the-answers world.

So you were never going to stop, were you?

I get it.

Thoughtless told me once that *human conditioning* was a wonderfully accurate and tragic term that was also a paradox.

According to Thoughtless, any form of conditioning creates unnecessary layers on top of what it means to be human.

'Being human comes first,' Thoughtless said. 'Conditioning comes second. Humanity is our inherent state of being. Conditioning is man-made; there are always agendas involved.'

If you ask me, agendas are always coupled with emotions. The two seem inextricably linked. Just like life and death. The only difference being that agendas and emotions change over time; death never does. Death is the same now as it's always been. I know that for a fact.

Emotions, though, they shift like the tides.

For example, things that once made me angry now make me sad. And, given that I spent years being mainly angry, I'm now spending most of my time feeling sad. I don't know why. I didn't plan it. Sadness somehow snuck up and snuck in. It feeds on the air that I breathe. It carries me like a lilo going nowhere in a pool without waves.

So I'm not angry that you rushed on. I'd like to be angry. I'd like to tell you that you're a fool. I'd like to feel that burst of red-hot certainty that roars through your system and makes you forget your own stress for a while. I'd like to, I just don't have it in me anymore. These days my energy is more wobbly, tear-laden panacotta than raging forest fire.

Consequently, all I've got for you is this, offered with the softness of a sad pudding:

If you rushed on because you've already felt your death start, you're lack of awareness has let you down. Your death started way before you first felt it.

If you rushed because you want to get on with the story, I'm afraid you missed the point.

And the point is: death starting before it starts and ending after it ends, is the story. It's the all-encompassing story. All the little stories we create and share and give so much attention to are like the fish and chips you buy every Friday. Death starting before it starts and ending after it ends is like the paper wrapped around them and holding them together. It keeps the little stories warm. It protects them in transit.

Death starting before it starts and ending after it ends is the only wrapping that isn't man-made. It's a universal law that preceded us. It's not the only universal law, but it's the only one that's relevant right now.

What's also relevant is that you've got here. Let's forget

the speed with which you've arrived and acknowledge instead that we are where we are. And, as there's no going back, it's time to tell my own well-wrapped little story.

It starts with Darius Check.

Or, rather, it starts with the RSPCA Inspector.

OK. To be honest, I don't know for sure when it started.

My best guess is that it started before I knew it had.

As for the ending?

Well…

The Cross-Over

Darius

1.

In the late 1800's Epiah Khan wrote, 'Time spent alone is a luxury to those who share their lives with loved ones. Time spent alone without such affection is a prison sentence.'

I mention it because Darius Cheek lived alone. His parents, aunts and uncles were dead. Until the morning of the 17th of November, Darius had not had a visitor to his second-floor ex-council flat for six months. He didn't realise he was serving a prison sentence when the day began.

The RSPCA Inspector called to investigate the alleged mistreatment of a monitor lizard. As Darius lived alone and had never owned a pet of any kind, let alone a monitor lizard, it quickly became obvious that they were both victims of a hoax call. The visit lasted less than ten minutes. For reasons that were not clear, the Inspector left his card.

2.

Darius Cheek died from a paracetamol overdose that afternoon, the 17th of November. Even a ten-minute visit is enough to remind a person how lonely they are. Worse still, as Darius closed the door and listened to the Inspector's departing footsteps, he couldn't help but wonder if the anonymous caller knew something he didn't. Perhaps there was a monitor lizard living in the flat? Maybe it wrapped itself around the water tank at night? Perhaps those late night scufflings were not the couple upstairs, but a lizard's tail? The only thing worse than realising how lonely you are, is the thought of waking up in the middle of the night with a bloody great lizard on your chest. It was a possibility Darius could not live with.

Some people, kids mainly, overdose on paracetamol as a cry for help. Halfway through the bottle they usually have a change of heart. What they never get is a change of liver. Darius Cheek understood that. When he was halfway through the bottle, he didn't stop to make a phone call.

He passed at 4.15 pm.

3.

He moved in with me less than three hours later.

We bumped into each other outside my local off-licence.

When I say we bumped into each other, it wasn't a physical bump. Rather, he stumbled through my aura. The newly passed are clumsy. Think of babies trying to walk and you'll get the picture. Shades have to learn how to get around without a physical body, just as babies have to learn how to get around with one. And, as you'll find out sooner than you'd like, it's not as easy as it sounds.

Most people don't notice when their aura is being interfered with. I always do. I'm a medium. By which I mean that I communicate with the so-called dead.

The thing that saddens me the most about being a genuine medium, apart from the upset stomach and disturbed sleep, is the fact that nowadays fake mediums are ten-a-penny. Mediumship has become big business. Covid-19 gave it a real leg-up. As one lockdown turned into another, fake mediums managed to worm their way into the wellness market by claiming they met peoples' social needs. If you couldn't get out to meet your living relatives and friends, fake mediums offered to hook you up with your dead ones.

The truth is 99.99% of people who claim to be mediums are not. They're con artists. They wouldn't notice if their aura was trampled on, let alone stumbled into. The truth is, the only genuine, honest-to-God medium that I know of, is me. [1]

And I hardly ever talk about it – to people, that is. It's a topic of interest to the Shades. I'm like the doorman standing outside what you think is the best-ever 5-star hotel. When you arrive, you might feel obliged to acknowledge me briefly, but your focus is really on getting inside. It's when you realise you can't find the door, that you come back for a conversation.

That's exactly what Darius did.

He began by apologising for stumbling into me. He expected to be heard - another sign he was new to the other side – so I accepted his apology and asked him if he'd got a minute. When he said that he had, I knew he was as confused as a Shade can be. Darius hadn't got a minute, he'd got forever. He just hadn't realised it yet. When I told him that I didn't know where the door was either, he became plain miserable.

---

[1] When I say 'honest-to-God', I mean it figuratively, not literally. The whole God issue is complicated, especially for a medium like me. I've spent years working around the fringes of this God-space, and it throws up more clouds of confusion than it does anything else. If you're a believer, don't ever think that you've made sense of the God-thing. You haven't. The Ultimate Being of the Universe is far too great for your mind to imagine or contain. And if you're an Atheist, although you're wrong about when and how life ends, at least you'll have fewer frown lines.

'This is worse than before I took the pills,' he moaned. 'Now I'm lonely and homeless.'

He followed me back to 5a like a lost dog desperate to be put on a lead.

I couldn't help but wonder how his arrival would be received.

4.

It was as bad as I had feared. By the time I'd closed the front door and we'd walked into the lounge, Bella was ready for war.

She was standing in the middle of the room, hands on hips, chin down, nostrils flaring. She glared at us both.

Darius froze.

I stupidly took a step forwards.

Bella bared her teeth.

I tried to smile. My mouth barely twitched. My facial muscles didn't want to be associated with me. I couldn't blame them. Given Bella's obvious anger, I didn't want to be associated with me.

'What the hell...' Bella paused mid-sentence, raising her right hand, pointing the forefinger directly at my heart, '...are you playing at?'

I forced my mouth to make shapes. 'This is, erm, this is Darius.' I managed.

'Did I ask you what his name is?'

'No.' My lips clamped.

'Did I ask you anything about him?'

Prise open. Force a shape. 'No.'

'So?'

Raise both hands, palms open in a gesture of submission. Feel shoulders shrug. Realise eyes are staring down at my feet. Pray that's enough.

13

Prayer is ignored.

'Answer my question!'

Mouth is as dry as Death Valley.[2]

'C'mon. Spit it out.'

Wish that I could.

'It's my fault.' Darius was suddenly standing beside me. His voice had that tone that says, *I'm sorry*, with every word. 'We met outside the off-licence. I need to be somewhere.'

'Of course you do.' Bella couldn't stop herself. She understood. She hated the fact that he was here. She hated the fact that we were no longer going to be on our own together, yet she knew what he needed; she knew how lucky he was to be in 5a. She growled and looked up at the ceiling.

I'd never seen a Shade struggle with cognitive dissonance before. It was enough to make my mouth moisten.

'Bella,' I said. 'Darius hasn't adjusted yet. He only passed a few hours ago.'

'How?'

'He overdosed.'

'Lucky sod.'

I saw her stomach tense. I thought of the wounds I'd never seen. I forced myself to keep talking. 'He doesn't know what death is,' I said.

Darius looked at me and then at Bella. 'What is it?' He asked.

'What can you remember?' Bella asked this gently, shifting from threatening to caring in the way that only she could.

---

[2] Arguably it's the hottest place on earth, with temperatures recorded of up to 57 degrees Celsius.

'I can't remember anything clearly,' Darius said. 'It was all such a rush.'

'It's never anything else,' Bella said. 'Death is a rollercoaster.'

'You mean that's what it feels like?'

'I mean that's what it is. Death is the rollercoaster that connects the universe.'

Darius looked to me for confirmation. I nodded my support. All the Shades I've ever known have said the same thing.

'It moves you so fast, it sucks your spirit out,' Bella said.

Darius frowned. 'Why aren't I in heaven?'

'You didn't finish the trip,' Bella explained. 'You fell out.'

'Why didn't they strap me in properly?'

It was the first time I'd seen even a hint of anger in Darius's face.

'If you can't hold on, you're not meant to,' Bella said.

'How do you know?'

'I took the ride,' Bella softened even more. 'I fell out an' all. That's why I'm here.'

A slight pause, then Darius said, 'What if I want to go round again?'

'You can't die twice. Besides, who'd want to?'

Darius thumped his fist into his palm. 'I didn't plan to be here!'

This time Bella looked to me for help.

'It changes,' I said. 'I don't know how, I'm not even sure why, but there'll come a time when the door appears. 5a is a half-way house. You won't be here for eternity. You'll be with your loved ones.'

Darius relaxed his fist. 'Is that the law?'

'Only if you want it to be.' Bella tightened again. 'I'm staying here forever.'

5.

I found out I was a medium at my grandpa's funeral. I was twelve, cold and snivelling, watching the coffin being lowered, when my grandpa – my mum's dad - sneaked up and pushed me into the hole after it. I banged my head on the wood and passed out.

Whilst I was unconscious, my grandpa explained it all. For some reason that I've never been able to figure out, it made perfect sense to me. I told mum and dad straight away, but dad said I was hallucinating, and mum started screaming and crying.

When I wouldn't shut up, my uncle Mick[3] told me I was ruining the day and that I should be more respectful. At which point grandpa thumped him in the stomach. I got the feeling that he'd been wanting to do that for some time.

Uncle Mick threw up all over the finger buffet. I shouted out that grandpa had done it, but the adults said it was the lager. That day was the first and only time I've known a Shade physically touch the living. It was also my first lesson about the loneliness of the long-distanced medium.

And that is what you become.

Lonely. Distanced. Removed.

I do have a couple of mates. Guys who have been going to The Frog & Bull for as long as I have.

I reckon most people would think of us as three drunk loners, drawn together by our addiction to alcohol and quizzing. They'd be right – but only up to a point. After an evening's heavy drinking, Stew Gardner can still do a twenty-minute, fact-filled monologue about virtually every topic under the sun. Whilst Bean Curry can be totally

---

[3] No relation.

inebriated, and yet answer the most obscure questions with a casual, alcohol-defying, ease. He's also spent more time than any other human being sprawled on pavements watching ants leap over cracks.

'And they never fall down 'em,' he says, stalling for time whenever Barry, the landlord, tells us we have to leave. 'Athletes should study ants, it'd make 'em better jumpers.'

If Bean ever appeared on Mastermind, his specialist subject would be 'ants and their cracks.' It would be one of the great moments in the history of television quiz shows.

I tried to ease the tension in 5a by suggesting that the three of us sit down and watch an old episode of Mastermind.

Darius refused point blank. He said that, after the day he'd had, he didn't want to hear Clive Myrie say, 'I've started so I'll finish.' It was a fair point. So I pushed quickly for us to watch the second half of Who Wants To Be A Millionaire? instead.

I switched on the TV and we lined up on the settee in silence, like three jury members who all wished they were somewhere else.

Larry, a bus driver from Hammersmith, was asking the audience to help him identify Guy Ritchie's famous former wife. Seventeen percent thought it was Mary Magdalene. Bella snorted her derision, stood up and left without saying a word.

'Where is she going?' Darius asked.

'Forest Road.'

'Why?'

'She used to be a working girl.'

'I've always felt sorry for the working girls.'

'Me too.'

'Why is she going now?'

'Old habits die hard,' I lied.

17

Larry said he was tempted by Madonna. Jeremy Clarkson said Larry and millions of other blokes. Larry said he was sure it wasn't Mary Magdalene. Clarkson reminded him that he didn't have to play. Larry admitted it was harder than playing at home. Clarkson told the viewers that they, too, could experience the difference and play for a million pounds. All they had to do was make a phone call. Eventually, Larry went for Madonna.

'Final answer.'

Clarkson looked at Larry without blinking and then announced a commercial break. Within seconds a beautiful young blond was explaining to us the benefits of sanitary towels with wings.

'Do angels have wings?' Darius asked.

'Not as small as those,' I said, as the blond pirouetted in front of her bedroom mirror in a skin-tight pair of white trousers.

Darius wasn't amused. 'I don't need a comedian any more than I need a quiz master.'

'What do you need?'

'A friend.'

Friends. A subject sticky as treacle. It's OK to have drunks for mates, especially if you like getting drunk yourself, but can you be friends with the dead?

Imagine that being the one-million-pound question.

'I'll play 50-50 please, Jeremy.'

'OK. Computer take away two wrong answers. Leave Jack with the right answer and the one remaining wrong answer... The computer's left you with Yes and No. Remember Jack, you don't have to play, but you can still phone a friend.'

'I'd like to phone Ricky, please.'

'Who's he?'

'My brother. He's dead...'

6.

'Friends give without expecting anything in return.
Friends know without being told.
Friendship is a language beyond words.'

Epiah Khan.

Darius and I didn't speak again until midnight. Then I stood up to go to bed.

'Where shall I stay?' Darius asked.

'In here. On the settee.'

'I don't feel tired.'

'No.'

'You'd think I would after the day I've had.'

'Not really.' If Darius hadn't been a Shade, I would have put my hand on his shoulder.

'You're never going to feel tired again.'

'Why not?'

'You have nothing left that can feel tired.'

'But I know that I'm here.'

'Yes, but you're a different *I* now. The *I* that could snore was killed off by the tablets.'

'You mean I'm never going to sleep again?'

'Not as far as I know.'

'Oh, no…' Darius stared up at the ceiling. 'Time's going to stretch for…'

'Yeah, I reckon it does.' I nodded slowly.

It was impossible not to feel sorry for him. Consider it for yourself. Try to imagine eternity without being able to take forty winks. Try to imagine forever without the bolthole of sleep. You can't do it. Right? And when you've first passed, you still won't be able to.[4]

'I'll get you a blanket, though,' I said. 'Bella reckons it helps if you pretend that you can sleep.'

Darius sighed. 'I'd hoped there wouldn't be any pretending on this side.'

I shrugged. 'I think you have to move on further before all that stuff disappears.'

Darius straightened. 'How do I get there?'

'The door that I mentioned earlier. My sense is that you go through a door to get to the next place.'

'Have you seen it?'

'No.'

'So why do you think it's a door?'

'Because a door is the most common form of entrance and exit. Now, I accept that it might not be the sort of door that people take for granted before they pass, but it still feels right to think of it as some form of door.'

'Ok.' Darius considered before asking, 'Where is it?'

'I don't know. I think it appears when the time is right.'

Darius looked round the room and shook his head as if in response to a conversation that was going on in his mind.

I felt obliged to try and move him on. 'Don't get caught up on whether it's a door or not, or what type of door it is. That's just my way of interpreting what happens when Shades move on.'

'Shades?'

'You guys. The newly passed.'

'Why do you call us that?'

'It's a long story.'

'I guess it doesn't really matter. Given the grand scheme

---

[4] So, if you ever say that you've 'slept like the dead', you're actually saying that you were awake all night.

of things.' Darius nodded to himself. 'And if there is a door, it does imply that there's a grand scheme.'

I chose not to offer an alternative argument. Not least because I need to believe it, too. The door I've never seen offers the prospect of peace beyond my sadness. If there is a grand scheme, it means nothing is as bad as I feel it is. This is all a storm in a teacup, and I'm over-reacting. I can live with that. It doesn't stop me from feeling sad, it just makes it bearable. I'm not diminished by being wrong. I'm just human. Along with the other nearly eight billion people I'm sharing the planet with.

'Has Bella seen the door?' Darius asked suddenly.

'No. Definitely not.'

'How can you be so sure?'

'A Shade only sees the door when they are ready to step through it.'

'I'm ready now!'

'You're clearly not.'

A slight pause.

'Why does Bella want to stay here?'

'Good question.'

Bella had been good at her job as a working girl.

On the street, Bella would be desirable, business-like, and hard in sufficient measure to attract and challenge. Once she was alone with a punter, she'd pretend to be overwhelmed by his sexual prowess. There are hundreds of guys who believe they're the only one who ever mattered to her.

The truth is the only thing that mattered to Bella was earning enough money to change her life. She dreamed of moving to the coast, of owning her own little Bed and Breakfast overlooking the beach. She dreamed of having a Maltese Terrier and a small, white car. Surely, she would say, surely that's not too much for a girl to ask for.

And then, one night she took home a guy who didn't want pretence. He wanted to kill.

Her dream died with the first thrust of his knife. Her body took longer. The guy never said a word from start to finish.

Which is why, after I'd left Darius on the settee, I lay awake like an anxious parent, waiting for her to return, knowing that I was being stupid and that nothing so bad could ever happen to her again.

As I waited, I wondered, like I always do, what that sort of pain and helplessness feels like. Inevitably, I then began imagining what could possibly be done to even things up.

I don't know who the psycho is because Bella can't tell me about him. Shades can't grass. They can tell you what happened, but not who did it or why. The physical world has to recognise and clear up its own mess. Which, if the current state of things is anything to go by, we're rubbish at.

Bella never met Ricky, my much-loved younger brother. The one our dad always called 'young man'. The one our mum never fussed over too much. The one who taught us so many things before he left.

Ricky was the only person I've ever been able to talk to about being a medium. Ricky was no more drawn to the spiritual plane than Jeffrey Dahmer was to veganism, but he was accepting.

Of everything.

He was born with a cleft lip. He never once complained. He started losing his hair when he was fifteen. Teenage insults didn't faze him a bit. At the age of sixteen he was diagnosed with osteo-arthritis of the left hip. It didn't put him out of his stride. In fact, that same year he started studying karate. Before long he was going to class three times a week and practising on me every other day. He became surprisingly good. He was as relaxed about that as he was all the problems he faced.

All I had to do was get used to the loneliness of being a medium, and I moaned like mad. My brother told me to be grateful. I told him to get stuffed. He said he'd love to, but he hadn't yet met a girl turned on by zits, premature baldness, and a cleft lip. He even managed to say that without a hint of bitterness.

Ricky didn't need to win the lottery, or know the million-pound answer, to be happy. He used to say that being a medium was my gift and not looking normal was his. I saw them both as a sick joke. Ricky saw them as blessings.

He said, 'Most people struggle to feel different. You've been handed it on a plate, and I've been given it on a palate. We should celebrate.'

Good old Ricky.

Not that he ever got to be old. He was twenty-two when the number twenty-five bus skidded on black ice on Carlton Hill, mounted the pavement and crushed him against a wall. A twenty-two-year-old karate expert without osteo-arthritis of the left hip would have jumped out of the way. Ricky didn't move.

The police said afterwards that death had been instantaneous. But I know he saw it coming. For most of us, the benefit of an instant death is that we don't know it's about to happen. Ricky had a second or two to wait for it to hit.

I bet he celebrated.

I left Darius downstairs and fell asleep with images of Ricky and Bella in my mind.

I slept like a log and woke at 9.30am with a pain in my gut. That should have warned me something bad was going to happen. Sometimes, though, you get so used to the obvious you forget to take notice and, besides, I didn't expect to see Darius perched on the foot of my bed.

'The blanket didn't help,' he said.

I sat upright.

'I couldn't feel it,' he went on. 'Well, not in the way that I used to.'

He worked his tongue around his mouth, then licked his lips.

'I think my sense of taste has gone, too' he said. He looked round my bedroom and sniffed vigorously. 'This room's bound to smell -'

'-Thanks for that.'

'But I can't tell.' He stood up. 'So, when you first move on, your capacity to pretend stays with you, but your senses go?'

'It's more complicated than that.'

'How so?'

'Well, you don't have a physical body anymore, but I still see you with one. And I can hear you. Most people, of course, can't do either. Yet, for all I know, another genuine medium – if there is one – might experience you very differently. I can't know to what extent my personal biases influence my perception of you. So, I'd be doing you a disservice if I answered like a quiz master who knows everything.'

Darius blinked. 'So, who am I now?'

'Ah! Sadly, that one is easy. You're like the rest of us,' I felt the usual feeling run down from the top of my throat to my groin. 'You're still waiting to find out.'

Darius moved over to the open door. He looked out onto the landing as if it was a foreign land.

'I want to go for a walk,' he said.

'Where?'

'It doesn't matter, does it?'

24

'It won't matter to anyone else, because no one will know you're there.'

'I've been ignored all my life.'

'I'm really sorry.'

'It still doesn't prepare you for this.'

'I don't think anything can.'

'Then how do we cope when we go through the door?'

'My best bet is that we lose even more of ourselves. When you've gone through the door, there'll be less of you than there is here.'

Darius considered for a moment. 'I hope the best stuff stays.'

I thought briefly of Thoughtless. 'I think the best of us is the stuff we find hardest to recognise.' And then my mind change direction abruptly. 'What time did you come into my room?'

Darius shrugged. 'Around three-thirty, I think.'

'And Bella hadn't returned?'

'No.'

Bella never stayed out that late. Not since she died. It took me less than a minute to leap out of bed, confirm that she wasn't home, and begin to panic.

Darius tried to calm me by making the obvious point.

'Nothing bad can have happened to her.'

'Nothing physically bad can have happened to her,' I corrected.

'But something else might have? Is that what you mean? As Shades, do we still really feel things, do we have emotions? Or am I kidding myself about that, too?'

'They look and sound like emotions to me,' I said, 'but they can't be the same as you had in your original form.'

'Why not?'

'Same answer as before – you're not the same as you were.'

'But we still feel something.'

'Do you?'

Darius straightened; his eyes widened. 'Yes. I'm sure I can. I just can't explain what.'

'Exactly.'

'If Bella is like me, if she can't be seen and her sense of self is now so different, why are you worried about her?'

It was a great question. The best I could manage was, 'In case something unusual has happened.'

'Unusual rather than bad?'

'Yeah.'

'Do you think it has?'

'I'm scared that it may have.'

'Maybe you're worrying too much. Maybe you tend to do that.'

'I just need a coffee, that's all.'

'Don't let me stop you.'

'I won't.'

Darius followed me into the kitchen. The kettle had barely begun to warm when there was a loud, urgent knocking on my door. For one crazy moment I thought it was a police officer with bad news.

The last person I expected to see was Bean Curry.

For as long as I'd known him, Bean's hours of consciousness stretched from twenty minutes before opening time to around 2am. Makers of breakfast cereal would have gone out of business years ago if everyone followed Bean's schedule.

He staggered past me, grey-faced and shaking, and made straight for the cans of Special Brew in my fridge. He drained one without pausing, belched a disgusting smell, and opened a second can for comfort.

I was surprised not only by his presence, but by his manner. Bean feigned confidence and control, even when he wasn't feeling it. He wasn't feigning anything right now.

'You'll never guess what's happened,' he croaked finally.

'An ant's fallen down a crack?'

'Not funny.' Bean's hands began to shake. Which surprised me given that there was fresh alcohol in his system. 'I had…I had…'

'What did you have?'

'A visit.'

My heart leaped. Surely to God he hadn't seen Bella? 'From?'

Bean's mouth opened and closed soundlessly.

'Who visited you?' I demanded.

Bean tried again, failed again, and then emptied half the second can. It did the trick.

'An RSPCA Inspector,' he said.

7.

God knows how hard the Inspector must have banged on Bean's door to waken him. And only years of experience dealing with maltreated animals could have prepared him for the smell of Mr Curry at that time of the morning.

Some people would argue that a professional with such resolve deserves a result. He deserves to save a cute, potentially cuddly pet, and to punish a heartless, possibly sadistic, owner. What he got was ten minutes of his time wasted.

The anonymous tip-off said that Bean had tied a three-year-old python into a knot. The Inspector insisted on searching Bean's flat. As he did, Bean questioned his knowledge of constrictors. It soon became apparent who the expert was. When the Inspector left, apologising coldly

27

for the inconvenience and, of course, handing over his card, Bean reminded him that a turkey was for Christmas not for life.

It was all bluff on Bean's part. Since he collapsed last July and spent several weeks in hospital, Bean has been terrified of people in authority, particularly those who wear uniforms. So, when confronted by them, Bean's defence is to turn the situation into a quiz of his choosing and exercise his superior knowledge. The Inspector was lucky Bean hadn't had several cans of Special Brew before the visit. Otherwise, he'd have wanted to know why the RSPCA didn't do more for ants.

Darius listened to Bean's story with his mouth open. By the time Bean left, with my last two cans of Special Brew in his jacket pockets, Darius had found it necessary to sit down.

'Who is that man?' He asked.

'Bean Curry. He's a friend of mine.'

'I don't mean him. I mean the RSPCA Inspector. Who's he?'

'He's just an RSPCA Inspector.'

'Who do you think is sending him after us?'

'He isn't after us. It's just a coincidence.'

'Are you sure?'

'Pretty much.'

I realise that, as confirmations go, 'pretty much' is about as weak it gets. Ultimately, it's no more use than when the 'phone a friend' says:

I think the answer is c) "Barnard Castle".

And the contestant, sweating, asks, 'How sure are you?'

And the friend says, 'Fifty percent'.

If you're only fifty percent sure, you're not sure. You're guessing. If you were in the chair, not on the side-line, and you were only fifty percent sure you wouldn't say it. Pure and simple.

Not surprisingly, Darius recognised my lack of certainty.[5]

'How sure is *pretty much*?'.

Fifty-one percent. And that's enough when you consider that Darius is a Shade and there are certain things he needs to hear.

'It's one hundred percent certain.'

'You don't look that certain.'

'That's because I still haven't had a coffee.'

'At least you're able to have one.'

Darius stared out of the window whilst the kettle did its thing, and I tipped a heap of Gold Blend into my mug. The first jolt of caffeine into my system shocked me like a defibrillator-wake-up-call.

Darius shifted his attention from the sky. 'I have measured out my life with coffee spoons,' he said mournfully.

'T.S. Eliot,' I replied, quick as a flash. 'And that's the sort of question that wouldn't crop up until at least the two-hundred-and-fifty-thousand-pound mark.'

Darius frowned. 'I didn't ask you a question.'

'Everything's a question, if you change the inflexion.'

'No, it isn't!' Darius asserted.

'No, it isn't?' I asked.

Darius ignored my smirk, saying instead, 'The best thing Eliot wrote was: "Where is the Life we have lost in Living? Where is the wisdom we have lost in knowledge? Where is the knowledge we have lost in information?" Brilliant, isn't it?'

---

[5] That's why you phone a friend rather than see them on a screen.

I flicked some imaginary dust off my tee-shirt. 'I prefer Epiah Khan,' I said.

'Who?'

8.

'If you find yourself in a hole of someone else's making, you are either careless or dead.
If you are in a hole of your own making, you are simply heading in the wrong direction.
Measure people not by how confidently they walk the streets, but how well they climb out of a hole.'

Epiah Khan.

The only person I've ever told that I was pushed into the grave by my grandpa's Shade, was Ricky. He, of course, accepted it without question. Bless him. If the no.25 hadn't skidded, he would have been a twenty-eight-year-old slap-head now. Today, the 18th of November, is his birthday.

Which depresses the hell out of me.

Literally.

I've been a chronic depressive for ever.

I was diagnosed only last year, but I can't remember a time when the Black Hole wasn't there. It can hide in the shadows for weeks, months sometimes, but a depressive can always see it, just changing the shape of the shadow's edge, just a blurred bridge between shadow and reality. Everyone is born connected by an emotional elastic band to their own personal Black Hole. For the lucky ones the connection is never felt. The rest of us gradually tighten the band, often without knowing what we're doing, until eventually the tension is so great it jerks us off balance and pulls us in.

To Hell.

I don't know if Heaven is the ultimate warden-aided accommodation. I do know that Hell is lonely and heavy.

Hell is isolation and realisation combined. You know why you're there, but there's no one you can talk to about it. No chance of sharing, let alone support. And the weight of that keeps you down forever.

Depression is Hell on Earth. Depressives know they deserve to be in the Hole. They're experts at blaming themselves for anything that has gone wrong, even if it's only vaguely connected to them. See, once you've been inside the Black Hole, you can never fully escape it. There's no such thing as a chronic depressive who's recovered. Just like you'll never meet a recovering alcoholic who enjoys the occasional half.

On my good days, I'm a recovering depressive. When I'm not aware of what day it is, I'm in the Hole.

And I'm nearing the edge right now, 'cos I should have stopped Bella going out last night. Even though, I've got no idea how I could have done it.

'I've never heard of Epiah Khan,' Darius said.

'What?'

'Epiah Khan. He's new to me.'

'He was a genius,' I said.

'So many books,' Darius said. 'So many choices.' He dipped his finger into my coffee. 'Damn!'

'What?'

'I was just testing.'

'Wishful thinking, huh?'

'In a manner of speaking.' Darius paused. 'I lived the last years of my life without ever recognising how lonely I was. My books were enough. Until that RSPCA Inspector called.' Darius looked out of the window again. 'Do you think Heaven's filled with spiritual counsellors?'

One of the strangest things I've had to get used to is the fact that Shades talk as if they still imagine, hope, and believe. And they still ask questions.[6]

I looked at Darius in his yellow T-shirt and black jogging bottoms.

'Most people would never believe you read Eliot,' I said.

'I spent my money on books, not clothes or food,' he replied. 'See, I never joined a library, 'cos I wanted to own the words not borrow them.'

'You can never own someone else's words.'

Darius raised a finger. 'You can if you digest them,' he said. 'Words are meant to be owned. It's monitor lizards that aren't.'

I remembered why Darius had killed himself. 'There's always a reason why people pass,' I said. 'Sometimes it's just impossible to know what it is.'

'In that case, it's impossible to know whether there's a reason or not.'

'I was only trying to be...' I gestured vaguely.

'...Reassuring?'

'Yeah.'

'It's not your greatest skill.'

My stomach twisted and the Black Hole threatened to open. I tried to talk my way out of trouble.

'Being a medium isn't a precise skill,' I said. 'I didn't go to college and study for it. I didn't sit down with my careers teacher one day and say, "I've got it down to two options, airline pilot or psychic medium on a limited income.

---

[6] Just not the questions we do. I mean, I really want to know why buses skid and kill cripples? Why a man stabs a woman to death with a breadknife and gets away with it? Why people you've loved and lost had to have birthdays?

32

What's your expert opinion?" This…' I gestured vaguely at my environment. '…This wasn't a life choice. When I was a kid running around in our back garden, using my imagination to turn a stick into a million different things, I didn't think I'd end up running a B&B for the dead. I wasn't planning to specialise in hospitality for the recently demised. And I certainly didn't want a house with an a) on it.'

Darius stepped back a pace. 'Have you ever liked yourself?' He asked.

Now that is one of the few questions that should never crop up. Even for a million pounds. My need for coffee evaporated. I pushed the mug away from me. It was the perfect time for a distraction.

The distraction was Bella.

'It's happened again!' She yelled. 'The man who killed me. He's just done it again!'

9.

After leaving the house, Bella had gone straight to the corner of Cranmer Street and Forest Road. It was the place that Doreen, Bella's best friend, had claimed as her own. The pair had gone to school together. They had shared their dreams. They had started working the streets on the same night. They had convinced each other it would be only temporary.

Bella had stayed on the street corner, talking to her friend, knowing she couldn't be seen or heard, until a guy in a black leather jacket walked up. Bella had recognised him instantly.

'Get away from him!' She screamed.

Doreen made as if this was the man she'd been waiting for all her life. 'I normally charge one-hundred-pounds an hour,' she lied. 'But you can have me for eighty.'

'He's the psycho who killed me!' Bella yelled.

'That works for me,' the man said.

'Excellent,' Doreen purred.

'Run!' Bella screamed, landing a kick flush into the man's groin.

'If you're good, I'll give you a bonus,' the man said.

'Baby, I'm the best…'

To cut a long story short, the psycho did a hell of a lot more to Doreen than he had to Bella, who went back to Doreen's place with them, trying everything she could to get her friend's attention.

Bella stayed throughout the butchery, unable to watch, unable to leave.

As she told me this, Bella's tummy trembled uncontrollably. If she could have cried, she'd have been hysterical. I'd have given anything to have been able to hold her.

'I couldn't stop him,' she said for the umpteenth time. 'I couldn't stop him!'

When the man finally left, Bella had no choice but to open her eyes. She wouldn't - couldn't – tell me what she saw, and I didn't push the point.

'There is one other thing,' Bella swallowed hard.

'What is it?' As I asked the question, I got the answer. Once again, I was falling into a hole of my own making.

'Doreen's outside,' Bella said. 'She has nowhere else to go, and she's scared to come in.'

10.

Without saying another word, I went straight to the front door and opened it.

Doreen was standing with her back to 5a. She was

looking up and down the street in an agitated fashion. She was wearing a short, black mini skirt and a black crop top. Her arms were folded, wrapped around herself as if trying to keep warm. Despite that, she was shivering.

'Doreen, I'm Jack.'

She spun round, moving back as she did so.

I kept still. I gave her time. She stood in the road and stared at me.

Then she said, 'Are you safe?'

The quizzer in me computed possible answers. The Celebrant in me took over. 'I am only here to help you,' I said. 'And no human being can ever physically hurt you again. Please, come and join us inside.'

Doreen looked me up and down. I gestured towards the open door. She whispered something to herself and stepped over the threshold. Bella smiled encouragement and applauded, her hands in front of her heart, as her best friend stepped cautiously into the lounge. Darius shuffled from foot to foot.

'This is your new home,' Bella said, as if she owned the place. 'We'll be here together now.'

'Who's he?' Doreen pointed at Darius.

'He's Darius,' I said, keen to reassert ownership. 'We met outside the off-licence. I brought him here shortly after he passed.'

'It was the RSPCA Inspector,' Darius spoke suddenly and quickly. 'He made me think there was a monitor lizard.'

Doreen turned to Bella for help.

'He overdosed,' Bella said.

'Lucky sod.'

'Yeah.' Doreen inhaled deeply and looked round the room. 'What do we do now?'

'We need to talk about who the killer is,' Darius said,

stepping forwards and sticking his chest out.

'What?' The two ex-prostitutes spoke and retreated in unison.

I'd never seen Bella take a backward step before. She glanced in my direction.

'Darius is right,' I said. 'We have to talk about the killer.'

'That's impossible,' Bella shook her head. Doreen followed suit.

'We have to find a way,' I insisted. 'If we don't, another girl is going die. This psycho clearly isn't going to go away and, based on what...what you've just told us, the killings will keep getting worse until he's stopped.'

'And who's going to stop him?' Bella asked.

'I was thinking that I could, maybe, you know, pass on some vital information. Anonymously.'

'Why now?' Bella's face hardened. 'Why not after he killed me?'

It was a good question. I glanced at Doreen and Darius. Whenever a contestant thinks 'Good question', they're really thinking one of two things:

1) 'It's a good question because I'm one-hundred-percent confident that I know the answer.'

Or

2) 'I really don't know how to respond.'

'Why do you want to do this now?' Bella persisted.

I still had more explaining to do. Life, unlike Mastermind, Millionaire, Countdown and all the others, sometimes gives you a second chance.

I spoke quickly. 'Like I said, if we don't stop him now, he's going to do it again.'

'You're right.' Bella hardened. 'But what matters right now is why you didn't say this when I was killed.'

'It's not a personal thing,' I said lamely.

'Really?'

'It's about numbers, not people. I thought it was just a one-off.'

'It?' Bella was like ice.

'I'm talking about the event,' I said, with as little chance of changing direction as the Titanic.

'It wasn't an event; it was my murder.' Bella's coldness towered over me. 'I was sliced open.'

Darius coughed. It was a faint sound. His chest had deflated. His edges were shimmering as if with heat haze. He looked as if he was starting to melt.

'We're falling out among ourselves because of what someone else has done,' I said, as calmly as I could manage. 'He's caused enough damage, let's not make it worse.'

'I'm allowed to be angry,' Bella said.

'With both him and me,' I agreed. 'And if you want to shout at me again for being slow and insensitive you can, only save it for later when we're alone.' I thumbed towards the heat haze that was Darius. 'Cos if you don't calm down, we might lose him altogether.'

Now it was Bella and Doreen's turn to look shocked; they hadn't realised the effect they'd had on a Shade more used to Eliot than butchery with a bread knife.

'Where will he go if he disappears?' Doreen asked.

'Maybe if he gets stressed enough, he'll go to Heaven,' Bella said.

'Shall we say something really sick, to see if he does?' Doreen suggested.

'Don't say another word!' I ordered.

Bella sniffed. 'Your left cheek always twitches when you try to be dominant,' she said.

We glared at each other, sharing anger like brother and sister. I told myself that I wouldn't be the first to look away. Doreen saved me from defeat.

'Looks like Heaven's been missed,' she said, pointing at Darius. 'He's comin' back.'

She was right. Darius had legs and an edge again. If he'd been alive, you'd have said he'd lost consciousness and was just coming round.

'How was it?' Bella asked him, ice turning to warmth in a split-second. 'Could you see where you were going?'

'I lost sight of everything,' Darius said. 'It was like I was drifting through a tunnel with no light in it.'

'You mean it was dark?'

'No. It was clear, but I couldn't see or hear anything.'

'If it's clear you can see what's in it,' Bella said.

'Like clear soup,' Doreen agreed.

'That's what clear means,' Bella confirmed.

'Not there,' Darius said. 'Clear's different there.'

'Where was there?' Bella asked the question we all wanted the answer to.

'I don't know.' Darius did his miserable look. 'It was just a clear place and I felt like I was becoming a part of it.'

'I always thought once I was dead everythin' would make sense,' Doreen said. 'Seems to me death's more confusing than life.'

'It's just a learning curve,' I said. It was a phrase I'd heard Paxman use once, years before on University Challenge. 'When you get the answers everything will make sense.'

'When do I get the answers?' Doreen asked.

'That won't happen until your killer's caught,' I said. 'That's what I've been trying to tell you.'

Bella and Doreen looked at each and nodded.

'If we start this thing, there's no stoppin',' Doreen said. 'You have to make sure he gets caught.'

'Or we'll hate you forever,' Bella said.

'At least that long,' Doreen confirmed.

I forced myself to look the two Shades in the eyes. 'I promise you that I'll get all the important information to the police,' I said. 'And I'm sure they'll catch him very quickly.'

11.

'When people talk about Intention and Expectation they forget that Intention alone lacks energy and precision, whilst Expectation limits insight and creativity. More important than either is Commitment.
In a field that lacks commitment, excuses grow.'

Epiah Khan.

'Nothing has to matter more,' Doreen repeated two hours later as we sat round the kitchen table having made no progress at all.

'I think we need to see it as a team effort,' I said for the umpteenth time. 'You have to give me something useful that I can then pass on anonymously to someone useful.'

'We knew that ages ago,' Bella said. 'But as we keep telling you, there's stuff we just can't say and do.'

Darius nodded. 'And I can't even open a book, so what use will I be?'

'The answers to this aren't in a book,' I said. 'The problem we've got, is how to get information out of you two without breaking the rules.'

'Can't be done,' Bella said again.

'Prove it,' I said.

'You know as well as I do that it just can't be done.' Bella shook her head. 'You knew it before I did.'

'Let's challenge it,' I said. 'Let's see if we can rewrite the rule.'

'The problem is, it's like there's a lock that's been placed

39

between my memory and my mouth,' Doreen explained.

'That's exactly how it feels!' Bella thumped through the table with the ease of a spiritual kung fu master.

'If there's a lock, there has to be a key,' I said.

'Is that Epiah Khan?' Darius asked.

'One of his earlier works,' I confirmed. 'He was wise beyond his years.' I looked at the girls. 'So, who's going to try?'

'I don't know how to,' Doreen said.

'Me neither,' Bella said.

I did my best to ignore their doubt. 'I want you both to see if you can tease the memory out.'

'It's not like the other memories,' Bella said. 'It's like…It's like…'

'Like something that's been locked in,' Doreen said firmly.

'Yeah! That's just what it is!' Bella nodded enthusiastically, as if she'd just heard something new. 'It's like there's a lock that's been fastened!'

'Right,' I said to them both. 'See if you can open the lock.'

Bella and Doreen were silent for a moment, their eyes flickering from side to side, both looking down at different parts of the kitchen floor as if searching for lost keys. They shook their heads at almost the same time.

'Can't do it,' Doreen said.

'Cos the consequences would be too great,' Bella nodded.

'What consequences?' I asked.

'I don't know,' Doreen said.

'Me neither,' Bella said. 'But it's definitely there.'

'What's the key?' I asked.

'Commitment,' Darius said with surprising certainty. 'You can't defeat a bad consequence without commitment.'

'That might be true when you're alive,' Bella said. 'When you're dead it's different - and this lock is still locked.'

'It's locked now,' I said. 'That doesn't mean we can't unlock it.'

'There is one other thing you need to consider,' Darius said.

'What's that?' Both girls spoke at the same time.

Darius didn't reply immediately. I couldn't tell whether he was enjoying his moment of control or was unsure of what he should say.

'The thing you need to consider,' he said finally, 'is exactly whose lock you are planning to open.'

12.

'Only a fool or a desperate man breaks into a stranger's home.'
Epiah Khan.

'You mean, like it's someone's house?' Doreen asked.

'Quite. Someone has taken the trouble to create and fasten a lock,' Darius said. 'Like you would if you were protecting your home.'

'It can't be God's place, can it?' Doreen asked.

'You don't need to worry if it is," Bella said.

'What, you're not afraid of trying to steal from God?' Doreen looked as if she wanted to suddenly distance herself from her friend.

'Nope,' Bella was adamant. 'See, even if he finds out or catches us, he's got to forgive us.'

'Why has he?'

'He's God. That's his job. He lets you off. He's like the dad who's too soft for his own good. No, it's not God I'm worried about, it's the Devil. I don't fancy breakin' into his place.'

'You don't think it can be him, do you?' Doreen asked me.

'I don't know,' I confessed. 'But I doubt it.'

'Why?'

'Because the Devil would leave everything unlocked. He'd want you to come in, just so that he could torment you. He'd make it as easy as possible. He wouldn't make it difficult.'

'D'you reckon?'

Bella was unexpectedly thoughtful, so I warmed to my pitch.

'Absolutely. If God's in charge of forgiveness, the Devil's in charge of temptation. Right? And you have to make temptation as easy as possible, or people would find something else to do.'

'Makes sense to me,' Doreen nodded.

'In that case, let's get on with it.'

'But we don't know how to,' Doreen said. 'We're still locked out, remember?'

'You might be locked out, but somewhere, somehow, you do have the key to get in,' I spoke with a certainty I hadn't felt since we'd begun the conversation. 'Epiah Khan was right – he's always right, that's why he's a genius – every lock has to have a key.'

'But I haven't got it,' Doreen said.

'Yes, you have. You just don't know what it is. But you do have it – both of you do. All we've got to do is help you recognise it.'

'How do we do that?'

'Get you to answer questions,' I said. 'As many as you can, as fast as you can.'

'Like on Millionaire?'

'Not really. There's no time limit on Millionaire and, to be honest, this is more serious. This is more Mastermind than Millionaire.'

'What's Mastermind?'

'A posh quiz show,' Darius said.

'Oh. I don't know if I'll be any good at that, then,' Doreen frowned.

'You will,' I promised, 'because you know the answers. I just need to keep you telling me what you know until you realise where, or what, the key is.'

Doreen glanced at Bella for support and got a thumbs up.

'Go for it, girl!'

'Can I cheat if I'm not sure of an answer?'

'Course you can,' I said. 'Bella will help, won't you?'

'Count on it.'

Doreen took a deep breath. 'Come on, then. Let's do it.'

'Right.'

I moved one of the chairs into the middle of the room and angled a light down onto it.

'Sit there.'

'Why?'

'It's Mastermind. I don't have a black leather chair, so a plain wooden one will have to do.'

'I'd look better in black leather.'

'Just sit over there and look nervous.'

'I am nervous.'

'It'll be easy then.'

Doreen took her seat.

'Ready?'

She nodded.

'OK,' I coughed, leant forwards across the kitchen table and began.

'Tell me your name please.'

'You know my name.'

'I know, but this is Mastermind.'

'You don't have to be very clever to know your own name.'

'It's not a question that's supposed to test you.'

'So why ask it?'

'We have to start somewhere.'

'You could start with a better question than that.'

'Just tell me your name!'

'Doreen Mitchell.'

'Specialist subject?'

'Anythin' I'm paid for, baby. I do everythin' better than the other girls.'

'In your dreams,' Bella countered.

'Quiet in the audience!'

'You told me to join in!'

'Only with answers if Doreen's stuck!'

'Everything always has to be how you want it.'

'Shhh!'

The audience fell silent.

'Right, Doreen, what is your other specialist subject – the one to do with keys?'

'Oh. That. Gotcha.' Doreen nodded vigorously. 'My specialist subject is...to do with keys.'

I decided to move on.

'Doreen Mitchell, you have two minutes on *Something to do with keys*, and your time starts...now!'

'Why have I only got two minutes?'

'That's the rule!'

'Doesn't have to be.'

'Why not?'

'Rules are made to be broken.'

'Are you good at breaking them?'

'Nobody does it better.'

'What's the secret?'

'Pretend they don't exist.'

'And?'

'And then just do what you wanna do.'

'How do you actually manage that?'

'Easy. You imagine the thing – whatever it is – how you want it to be without the rule getting in the way. You just say to yourself, "How would everythin' be if the rule didn't exist and what would I do then?" Once you've worked that out, you just get on and do it.'

'What would you do if the rule that stops you telling me about your killer didn't exist?'

Doreen fell silent, blinked, and began looking round the room as if someone was hiding somewhere.

'Doreen, I want you to imagine that rule doesn't exist. I want you to do that now.'

Doreen's head slumped forwards, her chin resting on her chest, her eyes fluttering.

'Doreen, do whatever you would do if that rule didn't exist.'

Doreen looked up at the ceiling.

'What can you see Doreen?'

It was as if she didn't hear me.

'Doreen?'

She moved abruptly, fixing her gaze on me. Her eyes glittered with a frightening intensity and a drop of saliva trickled from her mouth. I wondered for a split second if her head was going to spin. Thankfully it didn't.

Instead, she said, 'When the rule doesn't exist…'

'Yes?'

'…I say, *dat droll hen*.'

'You say what?'

'Bzzzz!'

I spun round to face Bella and Darius. 'What was that?'

'It's an imitation buzzer, it's easier to do than an imitation bell,' Darius said.

'Your time's up,' Bella said. 'Bzzzz!'

'Aren't we trying to achieve something here?'

'You said two minutes,' Bella said.

'That is the Mastermind rule,' Darius added.

'Haven't you two been listening to anything that we've been talking about?' I realised I was close to shouting but couldn't stop myself. 'Rules are meant to be broken!'

Darius shuddered. 'I didn't think you'd want to break quiz show rules,' he said apologetically.

'Dat droll hen,' Doreen said again, as if nothing unusual had just happened to her. 'That's what came out when I was...wherever I was. What does it mean?'

'I've no idea,' I said.

'It doesn't seem to make any sense,' Darius agreed.

I looked at Doreen, who clearly felt she'd let us all down. 'I told you I'd be no good at posh quiz shows,' she said.

'Maybe we should have tried Millionaire,' Darius said. 'Perhaps we should have a go at that later?'

Doreen raised her right hand. 'Look, if you want the truth, I'm rubbish at that as well.'

'Is there one you are good at?'

'I wasn't bad at Supermarket Sweep.'

'Yeah, I could imagine you on that,' Bella said.

And then it hit me, hard as a supermarket trolly in the central aisle.

'We changed shows,' I said. 'Once the rule didn't exist, we changed shows. 'Dat droll hen would never be the right answer on an evening quiz show on BBC2, but it would be a great starting point mid-afternoon on Channel 4.'

Darius was the first to appreciate that I was serious. 'What do you mean?'

46

'It's a Countdown conundrum. Well, technically it isn't because they only ever have nine letters, but that's definitely the game we're playing.'

'What's a conundrum?' Bella asked.

'It's a confusing or difficult problem or question,' Darius said.

'On Countdown it's always a nine-letter anagram,' I added. 'Which means it's a series of letters that you have to unscramble to work out what the original saying is.'

Doreen sighed. 'So the man who killed us isn't dat droll hen?'

'No. Yes. Well, maybe. His name might be hidden in there if we can just unscramble it correctly.'

'That doesn't sound easy,' Doreen shook her head.

'That's why it's a conundrum,' Darius said.

'That's why it's a crucial conundrum,' I said.

Then I saw the time and I knew I was about to be in all sorts of trouble.

'What have you messed up now?' As ever, Bella read me like a book.

'It's gone six,' I said. 'And it's quiz night at The Frog & Bull. Bean and Stew will be there already. I have to go.'

13.

Thankfully, the Shades were too angry to follow me out of the house. I left to the sound of Bella's voice shouting, 'I hope you lose! And remember, no spirit-door will ever have an a) on it!'

I'm sure she was right. What she wouldn't have considered, though, is that every time we close a door, we don't just keep something out, we also keep something in. And that's not always a good thing.

I looked around to see if Ricky was anywhere to be seen.

47

He wasn't. I wondered if he was locked out, or if I was locked in. Or maybe they're both sides of the same coin?

It took me only ten minutes to get to the pub. The boys were sat at our usual table. Their glasses were half-empty. My untouched beer had lost its head. I knew the feeling.

'Sorry I'm late.'

Stew waited until I'd sat down. 'Were you delayed because something funny happened on the way to the Colosseum?'

'Not remotely.'

'He missed an opportunity there to offer a rapid-fire pun.' Bean spoke to Stew as if they were part of a judging panel.

'And that's not like him.' Stew leant back in his chair, raising his eyebrows as he looked at me.

I ignored the invitation – challenge, more like – to come up with a quip. Instead, I gulped down half a pint.

'Although, to be fair,' Bean said, 'having a top-ten joke isn't bad.'

Stew nodded. 'Even if no one knows you wrote it.'

'That's the way I like it,' I said.

Stew didn't miss a beat. "KC and The Sunshine Band," he said. '1984.'

Bean tapped the tabletop. 'Don't let him distract you. He's trying to make us start thinking about the quiz instead of his joke writing career.'

'It's not a joke writing career – it's a joke-writing career!' I tried my best to look and sound like I was offended, but they knew me too well to fall for it. And I knew them too well to think they were being spiteful.

Bean and Stew have known for a long time how I earn part of my living. Apart from my work as a Celebrant, I get a kick out of being the unknown writer who provides some well-known comics with some of their best stuff.

The most famous guy I write for is Rennie Renton, aka The Pun Master. He's a TV star, quiz show host and filler of theatres with his one-man shows. This year, one of his jokes – one of *my* jokes – was shortlisted in the best joke category at the Edinburgh Fringe.

'Go on,' Bean prompted.

'What?'

'Do the joke.'

'Not again.'

'You have to,' Bean pointed at his partner-in-crime. 'It's the nearest me and him ever get to celebrity.'

'Even though you're an unknown celebrity,' Stew said. 'Which is as much a contradiction in terms as calling Boris Johnson a man of the people.'

'So, do the joke,' Bean repeated, 'add an extra line to make it twice as funny, and then go and buy the next round.'

I took another swallow of my beer.

'He's buying himself thinking time,' Stew observed. 'He thinks we don't know his tricks.'

'I don't need thinking time!' I said, creating a few, extra seconds by putting my glass down slowly and deliberately. 'Right. The joke is, I called my dog Creativity – which turned out to be bad news for my next-door neighbour's cat. And the extra line is, it's fitting that such a crap joke was number two in the shortlist.'

Neither of them cracked so much as a smile. Stew just shook his head sadly. Bean looked into his glass and sighed.

'I've seen dead pans with more emotion,' I said, before making my way to the bar.

Barry, the landlord, had the drinks already poured. Covid had nearly put him out of business. Social distancing meant that it was still going to be ages before the pub was as busy as it used to be. On the upside, the whole thing had frightened him so much, his customer service skills had improved slightly. 'Going to win again tonight?' He asked.

'Can't say for sure.'

'When was the last time you lost?'

'I don't know,' I pulled a face. 'I don't keep a record of our quizzing performances.'[7]

'Yeah, and I don't take payment for drinks.' Barry put my cash in the till. 'Have the boys told you?'

'Told me what?'

'Wee Drop's back.'

'You're kidding!'

'Nope. He popped in this lunchtime.'

'And had a wee drop?'

'Absolutely.' Barry smiled. It was as convincing as a Great White saying it wanted a cuddle. Still, at least he was trying.

'Thanks for the drinks.'

'That's what I'm here for.'

'Yeah.'

I returned to the boys.

Stew had the cards in two distinct piles face-down on the table. 'Barry being his new hospitable self?' He asked.

'He's having a go at it.'

'Pity it took thousands of deaths and the near loss of his pub to make him change.'

'He hasn't changed,' Bean said. 'He's faking it.'

'Fair point.' Stew raised his glass. 'Cheers!'

We all took a drink.

'He told me Wee Drop's back.'

---

[7] The last time we lost was June 14th. And that was only because Stew mistakenly said, 'Dylan Thomas', when he meant to say, 'Gareth Thomas'. He still hasn't forgiven himself.

'Yeah. I saw him on the Boulevard,' Bean said. 'He was on the other side of the road, so we didn't talk.'

'Did he wave?'

'Just a flick of his hand.'

'What else would you expect?'

We all grinned.

'Right,' Stew said. 'There's twenty minutes before the quiz starts, so we have time for a quick round of Sad Puddings.'[8]

He spread each pile of cards into a line and pointed at the one to my right. 'Your turn, Jack. Pick one.'

I tapped the back of the card, fourth in from the left. Stew turned it over.

'Oh good!' It was my favourite. It had a picture of a man's naked rear, with a red cross drawn over it. It meant that we were going to play a round of No Buts.

Stew gestured to the other line. Bean tapped a card that was in the middle of the row. It had on it an image of a laptop and a mobile phone.

Stew straightened in his chair. 'OK gentlemen,' he said with the formality he always assumed as Master of the Cards. 'These two have been chosen at random. The topic is social media. Mr Morgan, you are to argue about the dangers of the said topic. Mr Curry you are to adopt the opposite point of view. The rule is that the word "but" cannot be used at any time in the debate and must be replaced on all occasions by the word "and". Mr Jack Morgan, are you ready to begin?'

'I certainly am.'

'Mr Bean Curry, are you ready?'

'Born ready.'

---

[8] Don't ask.

'Then,' Stew checked his watch. 'Let's play Sad Puddings!'

14.

I began instantly.

'Social media plays a key role in maintaining, if not growing, most of the problems facing the world.' I paused just long enough to nod twice in support of my assertion. 'Social media encourages and enables the ignorant to become arrogant, and the arrogant to become abusive, and the abused to become marginalised, and the marginalised to become desperate, and the desperate to become manipulated, and the manipulated to become followers, and the followers to become converts, and the converts to become filled with aggressive certainty, and their aggressive certainty becomes the reason for their blinkered ignorance, and their ignorance becomes arrogance, and their arrogance makes them abusive, and the abused become -'

'- Ok! Ok!' Stew cut me short. 'We're not going round for a second spin. Mr Curry, how would you like to respond to Mr Morgan's opening comments?'

Bean didn't miss a beat. 'I would like to begin by acknowledging that human beings, for all their brilliance, have never created perfection – and never will. And, therefore, it follows that social media, for all its brilliance and the benefits it brings, will have some flaws, and perhaps even create some problems. And this is not because of the inherent badness of social media, bu…' Bean caught himself just in time. '…It is rather because of the ideological beliefs, egotistical, power-based desires, and cultural and personal agendas of those who use social media for their own ends.

'And it should be noted that Mr Morgan's comments were about how people use social media, and not about the inherent nature of social media. And that is all he can comment on because the value of social media, like all man-made creations, is determined by how people choose to relate to, and apply, it. And, therefore, the power is in our own hands, because as Steve Biko said, "If one is free at heart, no man-made chains can bind one," and that's the truth.'

Bean drained the best part of his pint without moving his Adam's apple once. I thought, not for the first time that, if Bean hadn't dedicated his life to alcohol, he could have been one of the great intellectuals and philosophers of our time.

'Mr Morgan,' Stew maintained his formal, Master of Cards voice. 'Do you have a reply to Mr Curry's comments?'

'Yes. Yes, I do.'

I flipped the mental switch away from my admiration of Bean's opening remarks to a swift consideration of how I could best use them to prove the point I had been saddled with. It's what I loved most about this particular Sad Pudding game.

When 'buts' are banned and only 'ands' allowed, you have to really listen to what is being said and then conversations build rather than clash. When 'and' is the first word in your mind, your attitude becomes one of acceptance, because you don't have access to the 'but' of denial. That doesn't mean you automatically agree with what you've heard, only that you must acknowledge it and use it as the springboard for what you say next.

'Mr Curry is clearly right in everything he says. And, in being so astute and so accurate in his assessment of the situation, he has, in fact, proven my argument for me. And

I thank him for that. You see, I didn't suggest that social media should be done away with, I simply observed that people misuse it. And it is through their deliberate and, at times, unintended, misuse of the various social media platforms that widespread harm is done. And that is why we should all be educated in how to recognise science-fact, communicate in ways that show respect, and understand the inevitability of consequence.

'Mr Curry quoted the late activist Steve Biko, and it made me wonder how many human beings actually live with a heart that is free from influence? It is, I would suggest, therefore, more appropriate to quote John F. Kennedy, who said, "Our problems are man-made; therefore they may be solved by man." And social media is a problem that needs to be solved by us before even more harm is done. And that is why I would -'

Barry the landlord's heavy right arm crashed through my concentration like a brick through glass. 'Three more pints gentlemen. I thought I'd save you the trouble of having to get up.' We all lost some of our beer as the glasses thudded onto the table. Barry appeared not to notice. 'Pay me for these when you come for the next ones.'

He was gone before any of us could reply. It didn't matter, though. The damage was done.

Stew glanced at Bean and then at me, before saying, 'Mr Morgan, please continue.'

All I had was one of my more recent puns. 'The Orient Express! The Flying Scotsman! Eurostar! Erm… erm…Sorry, I've lost my train of thought.'

'Thought you had.' Stew ignored the funny and raised his pint glass.

We all took a drink. Sad Puddings had been ruined, but alcohol had arrived. Not one of us was quite sure what our dominant emotion should be.

'When did you write that one?' Bean began the process of leading us back onto an even keel by 'and-ing' my joke.

'Last weekend. I woke up in the middle of the night with half a dozen new lines spinning around in my head.'

Bean's eyes widened. 'I don't know how you keep sane.'

'Says the man who has a thing for ants.'

'There are worse things that could demand your attention.'

'You are so right about that.' I looked into my beer and thought of the Shades and my promise to catch a psycho.

'Tell us one of the others, then.' Stew leant back in his chair. 'Any one you like.'

'What, so you can make a point of keeping a straight face?'

Stew shrugged. 'It passes the time. And it's -'

'-The closest you'll ever get to celebrity, I know.' I raised my hands in submission. 'The thing is, puns work best when there are literally dozens of them coming at you in rapid fire. It's the cumulative effect that increases the laughter level.'

Stew was unimpressed. 'I doubt that's an argument Michelangelo used when he first showed the ceiling of the Sistine Chapel to Pope Julius. I can't imagine him saying, "I know it's not that good on its own, but it really comes alive when you put it alongside all my other work."'

My two so-called friends chuckled, and I foolishly rose to the bait.

'Right. Here's one for you. Do you remember the good old days, when Baked Alaska was a pudding not a weather report?'

Unlike the Titanic, my joke sank without trace. I stood up and gestured towards the Gents. 'I'm going to the loo,' I said.

When I returned, the atmosphere in the room had

55

changed. There was a tangible sense of tension and hostility. I felt a little shiver run down my spine.

Quiz time.

15.

We won. Of course. Our performance was faultless. Even after ten pints and a bottle of Cabernet, Bean still knew that, for a brief period in its history, New York was named after an orange.

'When the Dutch captured New York from the English in 1637 they renamed it,' he informed all the other quizzers. 'So, before it was the Big Apple it was the New Orange.'

When Barry finally managed to get us out of his front door, we Boom-Ka-Ka-Chowed, with our arms interlinked, all the way from The Frog & Bull to the bottom of the Boulevard. [9]

There was no traffic – although businesses had been open for some time, every hour of every day was still Covid-lite – so we box-stepped into the middle of the road, where we spun round and round, going nowhere, like a snake with vertigo.

Eventually Bean broke the chain, and we all automatically began the who-can-walk-in-the-nearest-thing-to-a-straight-line game.

Each one of us claimed victory. Even Stew, who, without the support of Bean and myself, had collapsed next to the pavement edge and got two of his fingers stuck inside

---

[9] Boom-Ka-Ka-Chow: a mixture of basic dance steps, high-kicking and inappropriate hip thrusting, created by the same troubled minds that conjured up Sad Puddings.

a drainage grill.

'Spit on your digits,' Bean ordered. 'Use it as lubrication.'

Stew tried and missed. He tried three times without getting any closer.

'Fear not. I'll spit on your hand for you.' Bean started moving towards him.

'Stay away!' Stew jerked backwards so violently that his hand came free. 'And as a point of order, I forbid you from spitting on me ever, for any reason.'

Bean paused. 'Even if you're on fire?'

'Even if I'm fully ablaze.'

Bean looked at me. 'Some people just don't know how to be grateful,' he said. 'I'll see you both tomorrow. Boom-Ka-Ka-Chow!'

Miraculously, he managed a high kick that would have made a can-can girl proud, before weaving his way round the corner and out of sight.

Stew tried to push himself up from the pavement but decided against it. Instead, he rubbed his hand vigorously. 'I can't feel my fingers.'

'The blood flow will return soon.'

As Stew stared at his lifeless hand, I looked up and marvelled at the night sky in the way that only a truly inebriated quizzer can.

Infinity seemed oblivious to my scrutiny.

'It's so indifferent to us.'

Of course, even with the Universe, we are compelled to name what we can. It's one of the most popular ways we kid ourselves into believing we have control.

The International Astronomical Association acknowledges eighty-eight constellations in the northern and southern sky. I reckon the ever-expanding all-there-is-ness of the Universe must be thrilled by that. Although, if it's judgmental in any way, it's got to be squirming a bit at the absolute rubbishness of some of the more recent names.

How is it that the ancients could come up with such great titles as Orion and Scorpius and yet in the eighteenth-century people were happy to settle for Telescopium and Microscopium?[10]

I'm looking up and seeing something so mind-bendingly huge that my brain can't comprehend it, and yet I know it's only a glimmer of the entire thing. Meanwhile men-with-telescopes see a bit that no one else has and think that by naming it after something they use or created, they become eternal.

If people could see Shades and the space they shine through, God alone knows what names they'd come up with for that world.

'My fingers are working,' Stu said. 'But now the planet's spinning too fast!'

'It's always spinning fast. We just have to be drunk to notice.'

For some reason – maybe a subconscious awareness – I glanced across the road. There was a figure watching us from the shadows of a side street. I couldn't believe my eyes.

'Is that Wee Drop?'

---

[10] I kid you not. Telescopium and Microscopium are but two of the twelve minor constellations named by the eighteenth-century French astronomer, Nicolas-Louis de Lacaille. I'm surprised that, in recent years, Boris Johnson hasn't ordered one of his cronies to find him a planet he can name GotBrexitdonium. It would be a dry, isolated, place, with no chance of growth.

Wee Drop

1.

He told everyone that he'd been a history teacher for the best part of thirty years.

Well, that's not what he actually said. What he actually said was, 'I used t tea wee drop his.'

There are some people who don't waste words. Wee Drop didn't waste syllables. In fact, since he'd left teaching, he barely used them. To have a conversation with him, you had to know how to translate Wee Drop. Essentially, you had to be quick at filling in the missing sounds.

For example, when I asked him why he'd left teaching, he said, 'Kids jud les on wee drop feeba. Ca be d. Only wee drop lear is con, rest is sub. Nee more than wee drop pa and awa to und the ben of wha u rea l.'[11]

Which seems a profound observation coming from a man who is always a few syllables short of a sentence.

I mean, how do we ever know how much influence something has on us, whether it's a class, an experience or, even, just a thought? And how do we ever know when the influence stops?

I don't have an answer to those questions. To be honest, I doubt if even the greatest minds on the planet know the answer to, 'When does influence stop?' Which makes it one of those answer-less questions that can never be asked in a quiz. And I'm comfortable with that.

---

[11] The translation: 'Children judge lessons on a wee drop of feedback. It can't be done. Only a wee drop of learning is conscious, the rest is subconscious. You need more than a wee drop of patience and awareness to understand the benefits of what you've really learnt.'

As Wee Drop once told me, 'Aski qu, don me u wil fi th ans.'

Which has become one of those mottos I live by.

Seeing him now, tucked up in the shadows, comfortable as a puppy in a dark duvet, reminded me of something else he'd shared with me. Something I'd forgotten. Something I really should have remembered. It was, he'd said, the foundation for all successful teaching. Only Life was proving that it was far more. It was Survival 101. The realisation thudded through my brain like a hangover.

'You have to win the battle of the corridors,' I whispered to the Universe. 'That's what he said. You must be alert to the first signs of misbehaviour in the corridors and the playground, no matter how small, and address them instantly. That way problems don't escalate, and you don't you have to deal with them in your classroom. That means in your lessons you – and the kids – can spend all your energy on the learning process.'

I'd heard, but I hadn't learnt. I'd translated Wee Drop's words and I'd stopped there. Ironically, this time he'd given me the answer before I'd realised the question.

'How do you keep yourself and the people you care about safe?'

I could imagine the barest twitch of a smile scratching his face as he said, 'Wi th ba of th corris.'

And I haven't done that. I haven't even tried. Apart from the times I act as a Celebrant, I walk through Life's corridors with my hands in my pockets and my eyes down, hoping to be ignored.

'Right!' says the experienced, hard-as-nails teacher to their silent class, 'I need a volunteer to come out here and assist me in a demonstration.'

At which point ninety-nine percent of the kids become interested in their footwear. It's an example of what, when Covid was at its worst, people referred to as herd immunity.

Only looking at your shoes doesn't keep you safe. It shows your weakness. It marks you out as a prey animal. Just as spending too much time on your knees with your hands together, marks you out as a pray animal. Just as…

Just as…

…Sometimes I really hate puns. At best, all they ever do is put off the inevitable. Because, sooner or later, you risk a quick glance to see who the teacher's looking at. And they're always looking at you.

'Morgan! Get your hands out of your pockets and get your eyes forward! Now come out here and tell us all how you'll help the police catch a psycho-nut-job who gets off on killing prostitutes…'

When I looked again, Wee Drop had disappeared and Stew Gardner had fallen asleep, clutching a white line in the middle of the road.

I woke him up, and half-carried him back to his place. Then I returned to 5a.

It felt like I was walking out to the front of the class.

2.

Things had moved on a pace whilst I'd been quizzing and drinking and Boom-Ka-Ka-Chowing and staring and realising. The Shades had come up with a plan.

'You don't seem as drunk as normal,' Bella observed, her tone more dominant schoolteacher than complimentary Shade-sister.

'Stew mistook the Boulevard for his bed, so I, er, spent some time trying to see the start of Infinity. It had a sobering effect.'

'You were looking up at the stars?' Bella's dominance squeezed any emotion out of her voice.

'Correct.'

'And?'

'I was ignored. GotBrexitdonium was hidden behind cloud and Infinity couldn't even be bothered to wink at me.'

Bella refused to be drawn, and her abruptly raised hand stopped Darius from speaking.

'What did you expect?' Bella asked.

'You're right. Nothing, really. If anything started before it started, it was definitely infinity.'

'And why do you think it should have to prove itself to you?'

'Well…' I looked pointedly at my housemates. '…I can see and hear you guys, that ought to be worth something. And I wasn't expecting it to prove anything. I was just hoping it might, you know, show a bit of leg.'

'You wouldn't have known what to do with it if it had. Now sit down.'

I sat. The Shades didn't. Doreen and Darius flanked Bella, who took a step towards me. One hard-as-nails teacher, two teaching assistants and only one pupil. I looked down at my shoes.

Bella wasn't having any of it.

'Because you can see us and hear us, that's what I expect you to do. I need you to look and listen really carefully.'

I looked.

'Are you listening?'

'Yes.'

'With your full attention?'

'Absolutely.'

'Right.' Bella nodded. Darius and Doreen glanced at each other. 'Now, while you were out with your friends, we've been working out how to capture the man who killed us. It's taken us most of the night, but now we know exactly what needs be done.'

Bella fell silent. I kept my mouth shut. Bella stared at me without blinking. I raised my eyebrows. Bella glared. I looked to Darius for help.

'Ask the question,' he mouthed.

'What, er, what is it that needs be done? Exactly?' I asked.

Darius flashed a thumbs-up.

'It's obvious,' Bella said. 'It isn't enough for you to just pass on any information you might get out of us. Instead, you're going to go out and catch him.'

3.

The problem with that can be summed up in a single word:

Complexity.

Complexity is why headlines aren't answers. It's why simple solutions don't work. It's why the life-changing guaranteed-to-help-you-no-matter-who-you-are-six-step-process promoted on social media by the thirty-year-old with perfect teeth, is just so-much marketing nonsense.

Life is complex. Everything about it is complex. If you don't believe me, just consider your own body.[12]

You're made up of trillions of cells, a range of different systems, dozens of organs, and a skeleton with over two hundred bones. Your brain makes sure you feel loads of emotions and gives you the ability to think. In fact, it gives you the ability – or the curse, depending on your point of view – to have thoughts about your thoughts, and then to think about the thoughts you had about your thoughts.

---

[12] If you consider someone else's body, you'll probably get distracted.

63

Not only are you a mix of all these things, they mostly function without you being able to feel or influence them. You go to sleep, and your cells and organs and systems and all the rest keep on doing their thing while you're snoring and dreaming of winning Millionaire or The Lottery. You're not only complex, you have virtually no control over your complexity.

Your body is a metaphor for Life.

Complex and connected.

And that's before we start adding to the complexity by making all the rarely-well-thought-about decisions that influence our lives, and entering into the crazy-mix of relationships that are as shallow, deep, calm, stormy and ever-flowing as any ocean you'd care to swim in.

Think about it. When you're a child, everything is simple and easy. Even the hardest thing we do – which is learning to walk – is straightforward. We crawl, then we stumble, then we fall, then we cry, then someone comforts us, then we stop crying, then we forget that falling hurts and we have another go. Which we do so well that, before we know it, walking is taken for granted and we find ourselves being plonked onto a bicycle seat and encouraged to pedal.

When we're children, everything is simple. There is good and bad. There are heroes and villains. Light and dark. Laughter and tears. Tasty and spit-it-out-straight-away.

The term *grown-up* does not identify someone of a certain age. It just means someone who has accepted, and is fully engaged in, the inevitability of complexity.

And I am a fully grown *grown-up*. Just like the vast majority of you are.

Once upon a time, I didn't fear falling because I didn't cling on to my failures. Once upon a time, I had no sense

64

of personal identity, I wasn't worried by how different I was from everyone else. Once upon a time, everything was either tasty or spit-it-out-straight-away.

Now, I'm a Celebrant, psychic-medium, pun-writing quizzer, with no family but for a Shade-sister, and two brilliant drunks as my best friends.[13]

So, the almost inescapable grip of complexity is the reason why a simple you-have-to-go-out-and-catch-him plan, is of no more use than a skin cream that, according to seventy-four percent of eighty-three women, stops the ageing process. It won't. It can't. No matter how pseudo-scientific its name. There is no skin cream that can stop the ageing process.

I'll tell you what does stop it. Getting between a psycho-nut-job and his victim when he's intent on doing some serious stabbing. That'll stop the ageing process pretty bloody quickly.

I tried pointing that out to Bella and her teaching assistants.

It wasn't received well.

'You're only saying that because you're used to being a coward,' Bella said. 'It's a habit you've got to break. How often have we talked about this?'

'Cowardice is only one aspect of my character,' I replied, perhaps just a little too quickly. 'I'm far more complex than that.'

'Stop trying to shift the conversation.'

---

[13] And if you think that makes me seem unusually complex, just take a few minutes now to write down all the different roles and characters you are currently playing in your life. (And then, if you really want to risk swimming in Regret, ask yourself how many of them you wish you could change, and how the simple child turned into this complex *grown-up*.)

'I'm not trying to shift anything. Complexity is at the heart of the matter.'

'A knife in the chest is at the heart of the matter.'

Bella had long known how to rope me in whenever I tried to run.

'I'm still confused by the skin cream thing,' Doreen addressed me suddenly. 'If most women says it stops them ageing, who are you to say they're wrong?'

'Doreen, I'm sorry I mentioned the knife.' Bella's eyes softened as she looked at her best friend. 'There are just some things that need to be said.'

Doreen looked up at the ceiling, around the room, and then down at the floor. She clearly saw nothing that helped her.

It occurred to me that I ought to listen to my own words more carefully and draw from other aspects of my complexity, rather than just be pulled so easily into my eyes-down, hands-in-pockets avoidance strategy.[14]

'The skin cream reference has made me wonder, though,' Darius said, apologetically.

'Wonder what?' Doreen asked before Bella could get them back on track.

'If the ageing process has stopped for us?'

'Maybe you're reversing back to childhood...' I said it without meaning to. My mind flashed images of the newly passed stumbling as they learnt to move without their physical bodies. 'Maybe when we've been through enough of the right doors, there's only tasty left. Maybe Heaven is where there is nothing to spit-out-straight-away.'

'What?' Bella stepped back. The other two did the same. They all looked more than a little confused.

---

[14] Which sounds so much better than *cowardice*, doesn't it?

'I, erm…erm…Nothing.'

'What's going on in your mind?' Bella whispered, the venom in her voice replaced with soothing concern. 'You didn't mean to say that did you?'

I shook my head.

'You're going off on things again, aren't you?'

I nodded.

'What's making it happen?'

I looked down at my trainers. They were filthy. Bella knelt in front of me. She put her right hand on my knee. I would have given anything to have felt her.

'Tell me,' she said softly.

'It's complicated.'

Bella arched an eyebrow.

'I'm being serious. It feels too complicated for words.'

'What does?'

'The things that are making me feel like this.'

'How are you feeling?'

'It's like there's so much coming together all at once, like a perfect storm that surrounds you and blocks out everything else, and there's one big wave that's coming towards you and it just keeps getting bigger and bigger, until it's so big it blocks out infinity, and then it sweeps you up and spins you over and rushes you down and stuff gets in your face and on your skin…'

'Is that what's happening now?'

I nodded. At least, it felt like I did. 'And the Hole's just waiting to swallow me up, or it's reaching up to grab me. It's all going too fast to know.'

'The Black Hole?'

I nodded again.

'Have you only just felt it?

'No. It's been pulling around the edges for a while.'

'You can't let it pull you in.'

'I'm doing my best.'

'You need to go in the garden.'

'It's too dark. I need daylight.'

'What do we do until then?'

'Just keep talking to me.'

'I'm not a psychologist. What if I get it wrong?'

'I don't need you to be a doctor. I just need a distraction.'

'I'll do my best.'

'I know you will.'

'I've just got to work out what to talk about.'

'Anything will do.'

Bella nodded. Before she could speak again, Doreen stepped forwards.

'What's this hole you're talking about?'

'It's something he's got in his head.'

'He's got a hole in his head?' Doreen squinted.

'It's not a real hole,' Bella said.

'Then why is he scared of it?'

'It's a mental thing,' Darius spoke up for what seemed like the first time in ages. 'It'll be anxiety or depression, or something. It's more common than you'd think.'

'I thought you could get tablets for stuff like that,' Doreen said.

'He won't take any,' Bella answered.

'Why not?'

'A man's right to choose,' I managed. 'There are some things I won't put in my body.'

Doreen nodded. 'That's at least one thing we've got in common. Just because you work on the streets, doesn't mean that you don't have standards. I remember once, this guy asked me if I'd let him...'

I don't know when my eyes closed, but it happened whilst Doreen was talking. I fell asleep with the image of an irresistible black hole swirling through space, swallowing GotBrexitdonium before grabbing me and hurtling me into the darkness. I heard myself scream. And then, with a completeness that dissolved my senses, I was crushed into nothingness.

4.

I woke just after 7am. I was still in the chair. Bella was still kneeling in front of me. Behind her, Darius was trying to explain the significance of Eliot's poetry to Doreen. It wasn't going well.

'You see, what makes Eliot truly remarkable is that he was addressing man's relationship with nature, what we would now call green issues, at a time when few people were. And he was doing so in a lyrical, philosophical, even spiritual, way.'

Doreen sighed and scratched her shoulder. 'I don't care what you say, if it doesn't rhyme it's not a real poem. And if it's not easy to understand, that's just somebody showing off.'

'Great poetry is supposed to challenge us.'

'Nah,' Doreen pirouetted, like an over-sized ballet dancer looking for a way out. 'Prostitution challenges you, reading a few words on a page doesn't.'

'Why do you have to mention that?' Darius shook his head.

'Cos that's what I did for a living. You're going on about poetry and I bet you've never written a single poem?'

'You can study something without actually doing it yourself.'

'But you only know what it feels like when you've actually done it.'

'Reading and thinking are forms of doing.'

69

'You're kidding yourself.' Doreen sniffed. 'You see, what Bella and me both know for a fact, is that men lie to themselves. How do you know this guy Eliot wasn't, when he was writing his poems that didn't rhyme?'

'Because he was a genius.'

'Maybe that just means he was good at making you believe his lies?'

'Poets don't lie.'

I stood up shakily. The debating society was clearly grateful for the distraction.

'It's garden-time,' Bella said.

'Yes.'

I did my best to smile at both Doreen and Darius as I staggered passed Bella. It was once again abundantly clear to me why we learnt how to walk whilst we were still children. The smaller you are – the more comfortable you are being on the floor – the less distance you have to fall if you stumble, and the more welcoming the ground seems.

As I made my way cautiously out of 5a, Bella followed, ready to soothe my tears if I lost my footing.

Thankfully, I made it without incident.

5.

The garden knows nothing of the Black Hole. It's been my sanctuary from the first time I fell.

For all that, it's nothing fancy. Just a small rectangular lawn, surrounded on three sides by an abundance of flowers, with well-established white magnolias in each corner. The original brick walls are still in place, six feet high, providing seclusion and privacy. They keep the city out and let Nature in. The Shed of Necessity is tucked away next to the wall that borders the alley.

Since Coronavirus, every man and his dog has been

drawn to their garden. Now people are noticing what they've got, and what they can create. Now everyone thinks they're a gardening expert. Now, quizzers are having to get to grips with their perennials and their annuals. Now questions about horticulture are as likely as questions about history.

Some topics should be off duty to quizzers, and gardening should be near the top of that list. It's quite alright – in fact, it's essential – that quizzers memorise the names and birthdays of the love children of the rich and famous, but Allium Gladiator wasn't created to be a memory-challenge. I don't want to associate my garden with competition. I don't want flowers to become point-scorers.

This morning, as ever, the garden was doing its best to help me. The great thing about nature is that it attracts more of its own, and there is a community living just outside my back door.

As I stepped outside, the Settled-In-Sparrows were chirping their usual early morning greeting from the midst of the hedge that borders my north wall. Bright-eyed Robin was pecking at the soil between the hydrangeas. Two of my Protective Pigeons fluttered down onto the chimney of the house opposite. I waved a hand in greeting and smiled a smile meant to confirm that everything was OK. It was an unconvincing effort, and the pigeons stayed put.

I needed to have a serious talk with myself. So, I did what I always do in this situation, I walked into the Outdoor Lavvies.

Lavenders are often mistaken for flowers, but they are actually herbs. English Lavender, the variety I grow, copes well with the coldish climate of our green and pleasant land.

They dominate one part of my garden and, whenever I need to be drawn out of myself and away from the gravitational pull of the Hole, I spend some time standing amongst them. Their smell is irresistible. I always feel that they're reaching up, offering to draw me into their world. I always accept. They are so well-established, standing the best part of three feet tall, that I can take their scent on my fingertips whilst I look up at the sky. It's the perfect in-between.

Heaven and Earth.

Us, sandwiched in the middle.

The Shades somewhere else in the sandwich.

Or, if not actually in the bread, they are like the crisps that go on the side. Or the breadcrumbs that are left behind, unnoticed. I've never been able to get my head around just where the Shades fit in the Heaven and Earth sandwich. But sometimes I find that it helps to think of the Universe as an infinite Deli with its own, unique delivery service.

It's certainly helping me today.

Right now, in the Outdoor Lavvies, with the Protective Pigeons watching my six, I'm really getting rid of some bad stuff.

And that, of course, creates the space for something new to grow.

You always have to clear things out, whether that's in your garden, your house, your gut or your head, before you can install something new. Paradoxically, the Black Hole becomes most obvious and has the most energy when I'm cluttered. It's as if my uncontrollable swirl of emotions and thoughts are drawn in by the Hole's magnetic pull and the closer they get, the more violent and chaotic they become.

Out here, right now, the magnetic force is weakening at

a rate of knots. I want to say it's happening faster than it ever has, but I'm scared to think like that because when something happens for the first time, you can't trust that it's really happening at all. And if you talk about it, you really are tempting fate.

So, instead, I'll focus on the clouds and the Lavender scent and their feel against my fingertips, and I'll start with the obvious truth.

I'm a talker, a writer, and a question-answerer, not a doer.

I meet with people who have just lost a loved one. I learn some basic things about them, their immediate needs, and the life of the person who has moved on. Then I write a script that I memorise and pretend to read as I do my best to keep them moving through the grief process.

Another version of me likes to make people laugh. Well, to help comedians make people laugh. I've never delivered jokes to a real-life audience because I daren't risk their disapproval.

As both a Celebrant and a joke-writer, I'm incapable of accepting ownership of my words. When I'm in a crematorium, if I pretend I'm reading the script, I feel that it creates some distance between me and my words. If any of my puns fail when Rennie Renton is trying out material for his next show, I only experience it second-hand.

As a quizzer, I've only ever been a team player. Bean and Stew not only provide support, they also provide protection. They cover my weaknesses with their strengths. And, in public at least, they'll often take credit for what I get right. Which suits me just fine.

And then – and most important by far - I see and communicate with Shades. I know something super-important about the nature of life, and I've told no one, even though it would ease the pain felt by so many. I keep quiet because I don't want to be seen as weird. I don't want to stand out.

Yet a part of me really admires those individuals who do put their head above the parapet, who do accept ownership of who they are and what they can do. I think Rennie Renton is great. As a long-time quizzer, I'm thrilled that the best quizzers we have are now TV stars. The irony is that, although I'm a huge fan of the Governess, the Beast, and all the others, I could never do what they do. And now the Shades want me to go on an actual chase.

And I know that I should.

And what makes this worse than anything ever, is I know that I must.[15]

This time, I'm not resisting the Black Hole because it's so bad, I'm resisting it so I can do something that's even more frightening.

The Black Hole is infinitely preferable to chasing down the psycho-nut-job who killed Bella and Doreen. I know what the Black Hole is like. I've been there more than once. I know it's real and I know what to expect. And, most importantly, I know that, at some point, it will let me go. Right now, the Black Hole offers the security of solitary confinement in a prison I've been in before. The chase offers the very real possibility of a kitchen knife in my lungs.

And despite that, some part of me – some part I've never experienced before – is telling me that I have to go on the chase. Where the Beast will be real, the Sinnerman will really sin, and the Dark Destroyer will destroy in the darkest of ways. And there'll be no cheeky, Cockney chap

---

[15] That's right, worse than anything ever. Worse, even, than Ricky's death - and the other deaths - because I wasn't there when they happened. I'm going to be there for this.

to protect me.

Not only that, I've no idea how to go about it. I've no idea what my strategy should be, nor how to control the growing emotion that feels like terror's teenage brother. I mean, I haven't even started yet, I don't have the faintest clue what my plan will be, and already I'm beyond scared.

If this was the most personal of all quizzes, the next questions would be, 'Why are you, of all people, even thinking of doing this? What is your ultimate motivation?'

To which my answer would be, 'I'm not thinking of doing it. I'm going to do it! I'm going to do it because I'm the only person with a home that has an a) that stands for Access and Acceptance for Shades.

'I'm going to do it because...because of Bella. First and foremost, because of her. I'm going to do it for my Shade-sister.'

It's taken me too long, but I've finally stepped up to the plate. I need, as the Americans would say, to knock this out of the park. And the garden has helped me realise my first, all-important step.

I stepped out of the Lavvies, keen to share my realisation with Bella and the others. Like a fool, I looked up at my neighbour's chimney. The Protective Pigeons had gone. Teen terror grew another shoe size. The growth spurt made me retch. I'm not superstitious, but I do know what I know, and the pigeons have never deserted me before.

6.

The Shades remained silent when I went back inside. I guessed that Bella had told the other two to let me speak first. So I did.

'I can't do this on my own,' I said. 'Honestly, I want to

75

do this for you – I need to – but I can't do it alone. I just haven't got what it takes.'

'But you know we can't do any more than we already have,' Bella spoke softly.

Doreen and Darius remained silent.

Bella went on, 'We can't tell you anything that we haven't already told you, and we can't help you to physically get hold of him.'

'I know.'

'So how do you help us if you can't do this on your own?'

'I put a team together.'

'What?'

'A team. We operate as a team in here, and I need another team to help me out there.'

'I thought we were a family in here?' Bella frowned.

'We are,' I corrected myself quickly. 'But sometimes you need to go outside the family to get the help you need. Sometimes families can get in each other's way.'

'Can't argue with that,' Bella was lost for a moment. Her face darkened. 'Family isn't about the blood you share,' she said. 'Anyone can make babies.' Then she drew herself back and the cloud passed. 'But that doesn't matter right now. What matters is your experience. Or lack of it, more like. What do you know about managing a team?'

'I know nothing about managing a team,' I confessed. 'But I know lots about the value of teams. A team of quizzers will beat a solo quizzer nine times out of ten. And if you pick that team carefully, making sure their knowledge complements each other, they'll win ninety-nine times out of a hundred. That's why human beings are the dominant species on the planet.'

Bella considered what I'd said.

Doreen couldn't keep quiet any longer. 'We beat the

dinosaurs and now run the world because some people are good at quizzing?'

'No, it's because we know how to work together in teams to solve problems. That's what we do best. It's what separates us from all the other animals. We're not the strongest or the fastest, but we are the smartest, especially when we work together.'

Doreen didn't look convinced. 'I know loads of people who are idiots. You could put them together and call them a team as much as you like, they'd still be idiots. If you gave them a problem to solve, they'd just come up with the most idiotic solution possible. How would that help?'

'That wouldn't help. But that's not what I'm talking about. I need – we need – a team made up of people who aren't idiots and who can work together to be greater than the sum of their parts.'

'What does that mean?'

Now it was Darius who couldn't keep quiet. 'It means that if you have only one person doing a job, you've got only one brain working on it. But, if you get five people working on the same job, you get more than five brains' worth of brainpower.'

'How do you?' Doreen frowned. 'Are you saying that some people have two brains? 'Cos I've never heard that before. And if they do, where do they keep their second brain? Do they just have a massive head, or is it somewhere else?'

'No,' Darius sighed. 'The five people only have one brain each. It's just that when you combine their five brains, you get more than five.'

'That's rubbish. Five times one equals five. I'm no expert at sums, but even I know that.'

I looked at Bella for guidance. She shook her head, telling me to let this play out.

'We're not talking about just numbers, we're talking about the number of brains.' Darius was already beginning to raise his voice. I figured he'd be screaming before too long. 'If it was just a simple piece of multiplication, then you'd be right. Five times one does equal five. But when you're talking about people combining their brain power, it doesn't work like that. Five brains can combine to be more useful than just five brains.'

Doreen sat down. 'Where do the other brains come from?'

'There aren't any other brains!'

'So how do you get more than five?'

'Because the five working together are greater than the sum of their parts!'

'Which parts are you adding together?'

'What?' Darius took an involuntary step backwards. His body jolted and twitched like he'd just been tasered.

'Which of their parts are you adding together so you get more than five?'

'I'm not adding any of their parts together. It's a figure of speech. They're not actual parts.'

Doreen shook her head and ran her hands through her hair. 'So, what you're saying is, five brains working together add up to more than a load of parts that you're not adding together because they don't exist.' She looked at Bella. 'Why is he wasting our time telling us that?'

'Blokes just like to hear themselves speak,' Bella raised an eyebrow. 'They think they're experts on everything. Even though their brains are in their pants.'

'I thought they were the parts he was talking about.'

'There aren't any parts!' Darius threw back his head, like he was yelling to someone on a clifftop. 'There never were any parts! Never! It was all about brain power, not genitalia!'

78

The two girls looked at each other. 'Good job he's a bloke,' Doreen said. 'He'd never have coped with PMT.'

Bella nodded. 'No matter how many brains he'd got.'

Darius screamed.

7.

After that, it didn't take long to sort everything out.

Bella had, of course, been right. Doreen had needed to say her piece, to make sense of it all and feel that she was contributing. Darius needed to share his learning. They both needed to fall out, so they could make up.

By midday, we were all on the same page.

By 12.30, I was at The Frog & Bull.

Stew and Bean were at our usual table. Barry's niece, Morgan, was serving behind the bar. She ran the place during the daylight hours. She was one of the few people who always smiled as if she was genuinely pleased to see me. And I was always genuinely pleased to see her. We did our usual greeting. It was her creation. She always went first.

'Guten.'

'Guten.'

'Morgan.'

'Morgan.'

'How are you today, Jack?'

'I'm doing Ok, all things considered.'

'That doesn't sound too good.' She poured the drinks without asking for confirmation. 'What are the things that need to be considered?'

'Good question.'

'That's why I write the quizzes, rather than play in them.' She focused studiously on the pint glass she was filling. I appreciated the privacy. It made talking easier, especially in here.

'I'm going to have a conversation with the boys that they're not expecting.'

'Not sure how it's going to go?'

'I don't have the faintest idea. And...'

'And?'

'And the pigeons left before I did.'

'Did they now?' She slid two full pints towards me and started on the third.

'Yeah. They'd gone before I'd finished in the Lavvies, and they've never done that before.'

'You're seeing that as an omen?'

'I can't see it any other way.'

'Could've been something to do with the thermals.'

'D'you reckon?'

'Sure. There could have been a change in the wind that made them want to take flight.'

'I hadn't considered that.'

'Birds and the wind, they go together like lager and?'

'Lime.'

'Mac and?'

'Cheese.'

'R2D2 and?'

'C3PO.'

'Thelma and?'

'Louise.'

'John Eric Bartholomew and?'

'Ernest Wiseman.'

'Very good.' She presented the third pint.

'You saved the hardest 'till last.'

'My money was on you.'

'Thanks.'

'You're welcome.'

'Morgan.'

'Morgan.'

I'm an expert at carrying three full pint glasses and putting them down without spilling a drop on the table. Neither Stew nor Bean offered a word of greeting or gratitude.

Instead, Stew nodded towards the bar and asked, 'Did you get any clues?'

'She doesn't give clues.'

'Not intentionally, but everybody makes mistakes.'

'Morgan doesn't. She never mentions the quizzes that have happened, let alone the one that's coming up.'

'Never puts a wrong answer to a question either,' Bean sipped at his drink.

'Not even a controversial one.' I doubled down on the point.

'It certainly makes quizzing easier,' Stew said.

'Yeah, when you trust the question writer you can just relax and focus on your own job.' Bean tapped the top of his glass with his forefinger. 'It's like when you're sure of the drink, you can get straight into drinking rather than tasting.'

'True,' Stew nodded. 'It's like when you know the comedian's funny, you've got a smile on your face before they even do their first joke.'

They both looked at me.

'Oh, c'mon boys! I didn't come here to entertain you.'

'If you did, we'd all be disappointed.' Stew looked past me and over towards the bar. 'See, we're not sitting here with smiles on our faces. In fact, if anything, we're distracted by what's going on around us.'

I glanced over my shoulder. Morgan had disappeared. 'There's no one else in here.'

'Exactly.'

'I'm not here to share my latest jokes.' I made a point of

pushing my beer glass away from me. 'I need us to do something that we've never done before.'

'What's that?' It was Stew who asked the question.

'I need us to be serious. I need us to be honest. I've got to tell you something and it's really important.'

'How important?'

'Mega.'

'And this isn't a set-up?'

'No. There isn't a pun in sight.'

Stew looked at Bean. 'I haven't seen him like this, have you?'

Bean shook his head.

'You haven't seen me like this because, well, this isn't what we do. At least, it isn't something we've ever done together.'

'What isn't?'

'Behave like responsible grown-ups.'

'I gave that up a long time ago.' Stew looked at Bean for a second time. 'What about you?'

'I can't remember the last time.'

Something in Bean's voice made me shiver.

'I'm sorry if this is...if this is a complete deviation from the norm, but -'

'- A complete deviation from the norm?' Bean straightened as he spoke. For some reason my imagination flashed an image of the last seconds of Ricky's life, just before the bus hit. 'If whatever is going on is making you use phrases like that, you must be in a real mess.'

'I am. Well, it's not me exactly.'

'Then who is it, exactly?'

'Yeah. Who?' Stew leant forwards. 'You hardly know anyone apart from us, and there's nothing wrong with us.'

'You're right, that's the thing. That's what makes this...'

'...A complete deviation?' Bean's voice was coldly

inquisitive.

'Yeah. Complete.' My mouth was suddenly dry.

'And it doesn't have anything to do with that RSPCA Inspector?'

I shook my head. 'Not as far as I know.'

'In that case, we need to finish our drinks and get three more before you tell us about it.' Bean raised his beer. 'Here's to getting rid of the norm.'

'To deviation.' Stew clinked his glass.

I followed their lead. 'Thanks boys.'

8.

Stew returned from the bar with a smile on his face and beer running down the sides of all our glasses.

'What's the matter with you?' Bean asked.

'Morgan,' Stew replied. 'For a quiz writer, she's got a droll sense of humour. Very dry.'

'Unlike these,' Bean made a point of standing his glass on a beer mat. 'And now is not the time to draw a comparison between our professional joke-writing friend who isn't funny and a barmaid who is.'

The slight shift back towards our usual banter helped ease the tension in my gut. 'She was great when she worked in the garden centre, too,' I said. 'She introduced me to the Lavvies like she knew they'd be good for me.'

'I'd forgotten that's how you first met.' Bean inhaled as if drawing in the past. 'How you went from not caring about outdoor spaces to becoming a gardening fanatic overnight.'

'Gardens are good for your health. And it wasn't overnight. I had a lot of learning to do.'

'And Morgan, being a plant-whisperer as well as a perfect pint-puller, was the ideal teacher?'

'An enthusiastic and knowledgeable guide.'

'And with that said,' Bean played a drum roll on the tabletop with his fingers, 'Enough of this tittle-tattle, let's get on with it. What is it that's so important we don't have time for a round of Sad Puddings, and requires a surge of grown-up-ness?'

'I think it's going to require more than a surge.' It was my turn to inhale deeply. I tried to keep the past out, but it swirled through my nostrils and down into my gut, filling it.[16]

I tried to breathe it out as I talked.

'There are things about me – important things, I mean, really, really, important things – that you don't know because I haven't told you, because I haven't told anyone, and they're going to come as a bit of a shock. Well, a lot of a shock I suspect. And, erm, they're all true. So I need you to believe me and then I need you to offer your help with a problem that's, erm, really big. I mean, huge. Really huge.' I coughed. 'Is that Ok?'

Bean glanced at Stew. 'He hasn't mistaken us for psychologists all this time, has he?'

'Not us,' Stew shook his head. 'Yet it is one of those rubbish things about people, isn't it? They've always got the answers to other peoples' problems. They all think they can talk as skilfully as psychologists.'

Bean nodded. 'You're right. But none of them try to behave like heart surgeons.'

'Some people do cut others open though,' I said. 'That

---

[16] That's what the Past does – it fills space. And it's not only my past, or your past, it's everyone's. Someone breathes out their experience yesterday in France and by 11am it's in the air in Dover. There isn't a man-made border that can keep it out. Sometimes when the air thickens, it's not pollution it's the past. Sometimes they're the same thing.

is what some people do.' The tremor in my voice was as obvious as an earthquake. I coughed again and took a drink. The other two didn't move.

'Which people do that?' Bean asked softly.

'Psycho-nut-jobs who get off on killing women.' I looked down, but the table was between me and my shoes. 'Lunatic, frenzied sadists who...who do worse things than you can imagine and who usually get away with it because they kill women who don't count.'

'Which women?'

I put both hands round my pint glass.

'My friends.'

9.

Bean's eyes narrowed. 'I thought Morgan was the only female friend you had?'

'Sort of.'

'What does that mean?'

My grip tightened on the wet glass. I didn't mean it to, it just did. The veins in the back of my hands stood proud, as if they were trying to break through my skin.

'I have some other friends. Different ones.'

'When you say different?'

'I mean different. Well, in one way they're not, but in another way they're...'

'Different?'

'Very.'

'In what way?'

This was it. The two Jack Morgan lifelines that had run parallel for so many years, leaving me lonely but safe in the space in-between, were finally converging.

Here.

Now.

I was on the cusp. All it would take was one inhalation followed by a shaky, probably barely controlled exhalation carrying just a few words, a few seconds of sound. One simple sentence and the two lives would meet irreversibly at a single point.

My hands were gripping my beer so tightly I couldn't move them. The only route to salvation was if the glass shattered and shards sliced through my wrists. And that wasn't about to happen. If alcohol was ever going to be the death of me, it wouldn't be in such a timely fashion.

I felt myself inhale and hated my body for needing air. I felt my mouth start to move and closed my eyes so that I wouldn't see the words floating through space in their cartoon bubbles.

'My friends are dead.'

'We've all known people who died.'

'My dead friends live at home with me.'

My mouth closed. My eyes, still clamped shut, welcomed my mouth's decision. I felt my head nodding.

'Oh.'

I think it was Bean's voice, but I couldn't have sworn to it.

'In what way, exactly, are they at home with you?'

'They live in 5a. They go out occasionally, but most of the time they stay in.'

'They're dead, but sometimes they go out?'

'Yes.'

'And what do they do when they stay in?'

'They, er, talk to me about stuff.'

'You have conversations with them?'

'Yes.'

'And do you keep your eyes closed during those conversations, too?'

My eyes sprang open. Bean and Stew were staring at

me. There was an intensity in their faces that suggested they'd forgotten about their drinks. I took a swig of mine. They didn't follow suit.

'Who are these chatty, mostly stay-at-home, dead people?'

Bean was asking the questions with all the warmth of John Humphrys when he had chaired Mastermind.

'Mr Morgan, you have two minutes on chatty, stay-at-home dead people, and your time starts now.'

'What are the names of the dead people who live at 5a?'

'Bella, Darius and Doreen.'

'Correct.'

'What were their professions before they died?'

'Prostitute, unemployed and prostitute respectively.'

'Correct.'

'When did you first meet them?'

'After they died.'

'Correct.'

'How were you able to meet them, then?'

'I'm a psychic medium.'

'What the hell!'

I blinked. Bean and Stew were both reaching for their drinks. They emptied their glasses.

'Jack, what's going on in your head?' Stew's question sounded like a badly disguised accusation.

'Nothing. Nothing different, anyway.' I looked around the room. It hadn't changed.

'Can I ask you something?' Bean somehow managed to wrap a soft blanket around the hard edge of his curiosity.

'What?'

'Why did you keep saying *Correct?*'

'I didn't.' My eyes blinked several times.

'Oh.'

'Why do you think that I did?'

'No reason.' Bean and Stew exchanged a glance. Then Bean moved on. 'Jack, is this the problem you needed to tell us about, that you see dead people?'

'As in the film, The Sixth Sense,' Stew couldn't stop himself. 'Which was written and directed by M. Night Shyamalan, opened in August 1999, and starred Bruce Willis.'

Bean didn't take his eyes off me.

'No, not really,' I said. 'That's not really the problem.'

'Not really?'

'That's more the introduction.'

'The introduction?'

'Yeah.'

'To psycho-nut-jobs who get off on killing women?' Bean was working out the answers just as he did on quiz night. Only right now he wasn't looking pleased with himself. 'Before we get on to the nut-jobs, can I ask you another question?'

'Yeah.'

'Right...' Bean looked briefly at Stew, licked his lips, and then his words rolled out like thunder. 'Jack, how do you know that Bella, Darius and Doreen are real?'

10.

Really?

I mean, *really*?

How do I know that they're real?

How do I know that my Shade-sister exists?

How can anyone possibly ask me that with a straight face?

'I'm asking,' Bean said, 'Because, scientifically speaking, there's a great deal of evidence that suggests that dead people are actually dead.' Bean seemed impervious to my outrage. In fact, if anything, it seemed to be steeling his resolve. 'Dead, like the parrot in Monty Python. Only without the plumage. And certainly, without the capacity, or the need, to move in with a person they didn't know whilst they were alive. And, although I must admit this next question feels like a minor detail at this point, what exactly is a Shade-sister?'

Even through the indescribable mix of emotions that was racing through my system, I sensed that Stew was wracking his brains for a 1970's pop reference in response to the term 'Shade-sister'. I guessed it was his way of coping. I wished I had a way.

'She's Bella. She's my sister, but she's dead.'

'You never told us you had a sister.'

'I didn't. Not an actual one. Not one that was ever alive.'

'You're not making this easy, Jack.'

'That's because it isn't easy!' I've never shouted in a pub before. Thankfully, there was still no one else present. 'What part of this do you think is easy? If it was going to be easy, I'd have told you before, wouldn't I?'

As I wasn't really asking a question, I didn't wait for an answer.

'For all sorts of very obvious reasons, I didn't ever want to tell you or anyone else, but here we are. And for all sorts of equally obvious reasons, I'm not Haley Joel Osmont grown up and living low key. This isn't fiction. I'm real. And so are they. Shades are as real as the rest of us. It's just that at least the vast majority of people are blind to their presence.

'And I'll tell you why that is. It's because everyone looks at stuff and no one looks at space. Space isn't the absence of stuff; space is the home of stuff. Space is what *is*, stuff is what is created within the space. Human beings live within

89

the space. Shades don't. Shades aren't just in the space, they're part of it. They're not separate, like we are. That's why they don't start wars, or create political parties, or despise difference, or feel the need to improve their social standing! That's why, for all the things they still don't know, they're better than us.

'So, you can say what you like about me, but don't you dare – don't you ever dare - doubt or criticise the Shades!'

My mouth stopped as abruptly as it had started. My chest was heaving. I felt as if I'd just sprinted a hundred metres. Bean and Stew were wide-eyed.

'Wow! Where did that come from?'

It was a good question.

'I...I don't know. I've never heard myself think it before, let alone say it.'

'Better out than in.' Stew nodded at his own wisdom.

'Why do you call them Shades?' Bean asked.

'It just feels right. They've never told me that's the right term. They're not like us, they're not interested in labels. They've got bigger issues to address.'

'Like dealing with the afterlife?' Stew said.

'It's not the afterlife, it's only the life after this one.'

'Ok. I get you.'

'So, does that mean you believe me?' I looked at them both.

Bean answered. 'I don't think we've got any choice. Either you're crazy, or you really are a psychic medium and Shades really do exist. And whilst you're only occasionally funny, too-frequently sad, and by all accounts, a really good Celebrant, you're not crazy.'

'Can't argue with that,' Stew said. He looked round the room. 'Are there any Shades in here?'

'I can't see any.'

'Would you see them if they were present?'

'I don't know.'

'Hmm,' Stew sat back. 'That's interesting.'

'Actually,' Bean said. 'I think it's normal. I think, in this regard, Jack is just like the rest of us. He only sees who he sees.'

'Wow...' Stew stared into his pint glass. We all fell silent for a moment. 'He only sees who he sees,' Stew repeated. 'Is that profound, or tragic, or both?'

'It's Epiah Khan,' I said. 'He wrote about the danger of a casual glance.'

'But it's not a casual glance if you're actually looking for them and still can't see them,' Stew said. 'Maybe Shades are just hidden in plain sight?'

'Maybe nothing is hidden in plain sight,' Bean suggested. 'Maybe we just don't have the skill to see things?'

'Or the motivation?' I added.

We all looked at each other and tried to shake off the thought that people were wilfully blind.

'Or, at best, blinkered.' My mouth whispered without permission. I wondered again if the Shades actually looked the way I saw them. It's the only question I've ever thought of that I don't want the answer to. I need to believe that Bella is just as I see her.

Stew helped move my mind on. 'The most important thing,' he said abruptly, 'is that you are no longer hidden to us. We now know that you are, in fact, a psychic medium.'

'Yes, you do.'

'How does it feel?'

'What do you mean?'

'Now that you've told someone. Has it taken a weight off?'

I checked. It didn't take long.

'Nothing's changed. Obviously, I'm pleased you both trust me, but being a medium isn't fun.'

'Doesn't it make you feel superior to the rest of us? Or, at least wonderfully different?'

I shook my head. 'I'm not a happy medium.'

'That's a good line!' Bean grinned.

It took me a second to realise why. 'Oh. Yeah. Funny that the only time you find me funny is when I'm not meaning to be funny.'

'And you don't know anyone else like you?' Stew pressed on regardless.

'No. We can safely say,' I glanced at Bean, 'that I'm medium rare.'

'Suddenly the world is reshuffling back into its original place. In part, at least.' Bean signalled towards the bar. I realised that Morgan had returned. She began pouring our next round.

Stew wanted more background info. 'When did you first realise you were a medium?'

'When I was a kid. I, er, banged my head. When I came to, something had changed.'

'You're in good company.' Stew reached across the table and patted the back of my right hand. 'There's a story that the Buddha was knocked over by a horse and carriage whilst walking down the middle of a road. Turns out his enlightenment was the result of a concussion rather than cosmic insight.'

I didn't know how to follow that.

Bean did. 'So now that we've established, and accepted, that you're a psychic medium who shares his home with Shades, let's move on to the other detail. What do psycho-nut-jobs have to do with anything?'

11.

Before I could answer, Morgan arrived with our drinks. Her presence created one of those awkward pauses that people fill with forced, patently fake, everyday conversation. Stew provided that. I smiled what felt like a very weak 'thank you' as my glass was placed in front of me. Bean dropped his chin onto his chest and kept his gaze down, like a dethroned king waiting for the guillotine to release.

Morgan returned my smile, informed Stew that her day was going well, and resisted asking Bean if he was alright. I waited until she was back behind the bar before speaking.

'I think it's only one psycho-nut-job. At least, I bloody hope it is. History doesn't suggest that they hunt in packs, so if we've got more than one to deal with, we'd be as unlucky as a Ruppell's griffon vulture that's afraid of heights.'

'If it's afraid of heights, it isn't a Ruppell's griffon vulture,' Bean said. 'Which, as we all know flies higher than any other bird.'

'One's been recorded at thirty-seven thousand feet,' Stew said. 'That's more or less the cruising altitude of most commercial aircraft.'

'With that out of the way,' Bean said. 'Let's see if we can get back to the shockingly unusual topic at hand. Now, as I understand things, neither Stew nor myself have got a psycho-nut-job that we have to deal with anywhere in our personal landscape. The thing is, you seem to be suggesting that we have. And that is far more concerning than the thought of a bird – any bird – suffering from acrophobia.'

'Phobias can be devastating,' I said, as if buying myself a few more pun-filled seconds would change anything. 'Surely you wouldn't tell a person suffering from astraphobia -'

'- Fear of thunder and lightning,' Stew interjected.

'- That it's just a storm in a teacup?'

'Stop it.' Bean ordered.

'Or a person suffering from trypanophobia -'

'- Fear of injections,' Stew said.

'- That finding a cure would be like looking for a needle in a haystack?'

'Stop it.' Bean said again.

'Please tell me you wouldn't suggest that the best way to raise money for research into enochlophobia - '

' - Fear of large groups,' Stew said.

' — Is through crowdfunding?'

'Stop it!' Bean thumped the tabletop. 'This isn't about you making it as easy as possible for yourself, this is about you telling us what is going on. Some days are very different from others, so if this is going to be one of those, let's get on with it!'

'Right. Sorry.' I swallowed, reminded myself why I was doing this, and stepped off a cliff for the second time in half an hour. 'The thing is — the very big thing is — that both Bella, my Shade sister, and Doreen, her best friend, were killed by the same psycho-nut-job. And when I say killed, I mean really...' I waved a hand ineffectively above our glasses.

'Killed?' Stew offered the easy ending.

My hand clenched into a fist. 'Savagely.'

'Oh.'

I gave them a minute to do whatever they needed to with that. Then I added all the other necessary elements of the story.

Bean and Stew were vaguely aware of Bella's murder. It had received a mention in the local media, and they'd both clocked it when they'd done their daily trawl for anything that might turn into a quiz question.

Bella's death had warranted only a brief paragraph in the local paper and less than sixty seconds on the local TV news programme. The headline that day had been about an American Insurance company that had secretly advised the government how to run the NHS during the pandemic. A leaked report claimed that the company already owned thirty-five percent of NHS services. That was a story we were all fully aware of. It had been the media focus, for all-but the right-wing press, for the best part of a week.

'The NHS shouldn't be for sale,' Stew said.

'Women shouldn't be for sale,' I said.

'Neither should be for sale.' Bean brought us to agreement and then moved us on. 'So,' he pointed his finger at me, 'What you're saying is that if you mutilate and murder a prostitute, you're far more likely to stay beneath the radar, attract little media or, even, police attention, than if you did the same thing to a suburban housewife with two children?'

'It seems that way. As far as I can tell, the police are doing very little about either the death of Bella or Doreen. What makes it even worse, they told me that some other girls have disappeared during the last year, and these have all gone unreported. That means we have a serial killer on the loose and the authorities aren't looking for him. Logically, it's only a matter of time before he does it again. And, as he was even more violent with Doreen than he was with Bella, I think his attacks are going to get worse. Not that I can imagine how.'

'Don't try.' Bean frowned. 'The situation is undoubtedly tragic, and the girls are blessed to have found you after their awful deaths. The thing is, I still don't see what it has to do with us.' His hand flicked in the direction of Stew. 'From what you've made clear, neither of us could see or talk to the girls. And we're not exactly the sort of high-profile, influential citizens who can stir up media interest or put pressure on the police. So, why have you broken cover after all this time and told us everything?'

'Because I'm going to go after the psycho-nut-job. I'm going to catch him before he kills another working girl. I've made a commitment. I've stepped over a line and there's no turning back. There's no looking down at my shoes or putting my hands in my pockets. I promised Bella and Doreen that I would do this and do this is what I'm going to do.'

Bean was silent for a moment. Then he said, 'You're reminding me of that routine you wrote about those TV programmes that focus on couples tackling massively complex building renovations.'

'Oh yeah,' Stew nodded enthusiastically. 'We said to you at the time that you should consider writing more routines and fewer puns.'

'That's not the point,' Bean returned to his John Humphrys approach. 'Do you remember how that routine went?'

'Yes.'

'Remind us.'

'Really?'

'Yes.'

'Now?'

'Yes.'

'Really?'

'It's relevant.'

I felt myself caught in the glare of the spotlight. The words tumbled out of my mouth in my best Kevin

McCloud impersonation.[17]

'Peter and Patricia Pringle, have decided to leave city living behind and start a new life in the country. They've bought a small woodland area in the northern-most part of the Outer Hebrides. They're planning to build a tree house that connects 13 trees in an interconnected maze of corridors and rooms.

'Peter, an accountant who hasn't done a day's physical labour in his life, has designed a home amongst the trees that includes 7 bedrooms, 12 bathrooms, a massive open-plan kitchen-diner, a sauna, a cinema, a ten-pin bowling alley and an indoor pool. Patricia, who's run a knitting club for the last 15 years, is going to project manage the build even though she hasn't project managed anything more complex than a meat and two veg Sunday lunch. Peter, who's clearly a selfish and lazy so-and-so, is staying behind in their London 4-bed detached to oversee the selling of that property.

'I met Patricia on the edge of their woodland on a bitterly cold Monday morning in the first week of April. I asked her how long she thought the build would take.

'We expect to be in by the weekend,' she replied. 'Hopefully in time for Sunday lunch.'

'And how much do you estimate the entire project will cost, including fixtures and fittings?'

'Fifty-seven pounds and fifty pence,' she said confidently. 'Although we do have a contingency of an additional five pounds and twenty pence.'

'When I suggested that, in my expert opinion, they would need more time, money, and professional help,

---

[17] It's a rubbish impersonation. I sound more like Kevin the Minion than Kevin McCloud.

Patricia shared a knowing wink.

'That's because you don't know me when I get going,' she said. 'I'm approaching this project just as I would the creation of a winter scarf for an elderly relative. When my creative juices are flowing, no one can knit-one, purl-one faster than me.'

'I returned to the Hebrides 7 months later, in the middle of winter, to see if the amazing treehouse was complete. It wasn't. In fact, the woodland hadn't changed at all, and the land was now covered in thick snow. Patricia was living at the foot of a tree. She had obviously tried to build a shelter out of leaves and twigs, but the Hebridean weather had long since dismantled that. She'd lost 4 stone in weight, and her hair had got more stuff in it than the shelter probably ever had. Back in London, Peter had sold their detached home and moved into a Dockland penthouse with a 25-year-old Norwegian student.

'Patricia was shivering so violently she could barely talk.

'W...Why didn't y...you...h...help me?' She managed.

'I did,' I replied. 'I told you that you didn't have any of the resources you needed, and that you needed a professional to run the project. On a positive note, though...'

'Y...Yes?'

'It's misguided amateurs like you that have kept me on the tele for years...'

I realised as I recounted the routine the point that Bean was making. However, he clearly wasn't prepared to leave that to chance.

'Police work of any kind isn't a job for a misguided amateur,' he said. 'Going after a psycho-nut-job isn't something that even a highly skilled police officer would do on their own. It requires a team, going at it full-time. So, no matter how much you care for Bella and Doreen, you should forget this completely. Otherwise, you'll become your own version of Patricia Pringle.'

'You're right. You're absolutely right.' I straightened in my chair. 'I'm acutely aware of my limitations, and I accept that this isn't a one-man job.'

Bean saw what was coming faster than Stew. 'Jack, you can't be serious?'

'Completely. You said it yourself, this requires a team. So, I'm asking you two to help me.'

12.

Bean didn't return Stew's immediate glance. He just kept his focus on me.

'That's a crazy idea,' he said. 'We'd be a team of misguided amateurs. The saying, "Too many cooks can spoil the broth" becomes even more true when the cooks aren't actually cooks, and the broth is a matter of life and death.'

'There's another, more philosophical point that should also be considered,' Stew said.

'Which is?' Bean and I asked the question in unison.

'If, as you said earlier, there isn't an actual afterlife, there's just the continuation of life after this one, then killers are not actually ending anything, are they? Which means that, although they need to be caught and punished, they're not actually committing the crime we're accusing them of.'

'This isn't the time for philosophical debate,' I said, doing my best to hold back a sudden rush of anger. 'And I'll tell you why. Firstly, killers don't know that life continues after this, so they do believe they are ending someone's existence. And, secondly, even if they did know, they still don't have the right to choose!'

I heard what sounded like a growl at the back of my throat. Stew sat back in his chair. He swallowed and blinked. I remembered how quickly my Shade-sister could switch from anger to softness or anything in-between. I needed to follow her lead.

'Think of it this way,' I said as gently as I could manage. 'Nottingham and Leicester are closely connected, but if someone wants to be in Nottingham, they shouldn't be forced to go to Leicester.'

'You mean, Nottingham is life, and Leicester is death?'

'Metaphorically.'

'Dunno about metaphorically,' Bean said. 'I went to a stag-do once in Leicester...'

Stew ignored him. 'So, you can't be forced to go from Leicester to Nottingham?'

'What?'

'You can't be forced to go from death back into life?'

'No! Well, I don't know. The Shades I meet are all going one way.'

'So, reincarnation doesn't exist?'

'I've had no experience that it does.'

'Then existence, in all its forms, is a one-way road?'

'I think so.'

'There are definitely no roundabouts?'

'As far as I can tell.'

'How about lanes for overtaking?'

'What?'

'Lanes that enable you to go at different speeds. Does the one-way road enable people to travel at their own pace, maybe even break the speed limit?'

'Stew, I've never received any indication that life after this is a like a road. If anything, I get the sense it's spiral rather than linear.'

'Our next life is less like the M1 and more like Spaghetti

Junction?'

'If that makes you happy, yes.'

'It does, because...' Stew's eyes widened as they always did when he was about to score the winning point. '...Because spirals incorporate circles, just like Spaghetti Junction does, and there are scientists who argue that the Universe is curved and closes in on itself like a sphere. Which means that, if you travelled far enough through the Universe, you'd end up back where you started. Just like you would on Spaghetti Junction. Which means that reincarnation is inevitable.' He sat forward and raised his glass. 'I've always thought it was.'

'For God's sake.' Bean breathed out. 'We're having the most important conversation we've ever shared. One way or another this is going to affect us all going forwards. Possibly really seriously. Given that, let's imagine, can we, that we've all just gone forwards, in the fastest lane possible, to the end of the Universe and, lo and behold, we're now back where we began: with Jack wanting us to risk our lives by going after a psycho-nut-job. Can we all imagine that?' He looked pointedly at Stew. 'Can we please avoid any temptation to wonder if stars act as cats' eyes in the highways of the Universe, and can we explain to Jack, in ways that are compelling and irresistible, why neither we, nor he, should play at being detectives?'

'Ok.' Stew pursed his lips. We both waited for him to consider. 'I can't think of any,' he said finally.

'You can't think of any what?' Bean asked.

'Compelling and irresistible reasons why all three of us shouldn't play at being detectives.'

'Are you mad?' Bean jerked bolt upright in a way he very rarely did. 'You can't play at being a detective! The Pringles played at house building, and what should have been a joyous, creative experience turned into something terrible. What Jack's talking about is already terrible. We don't have any relevant experience or any of the necessary skills, so why do you think we should even attempt to help?'

Stew shrugged. 'It's the right thing to do.'

'It would be the right thing to do if we had the necessary skills and experience.'

'We can learn them on the job.'

'We can't! What'll happen is, we'll end up freezing our bits off living at the foot of a tree!'

'If my bits were frozen off, rather than cut off by a psycho-nut-job, I'd take that as a result,' I said. 'In fact, if losing my bits is the price I pay to see this through, it's one I'm willing to make. I'm barely aware that they exist, anyway.'

The fact that I heard myself say that was surprising. The fact that I absolutely meant it, was even more so. The other two heard it in my voice.

'It is a small price,' Stew said.

'Speak for yourself,' Bean replied.

'That's all any of us can do,' I said. 'Especially about this.'

'He's right,' Stew said. 'I'm in.'

'That's two of us, then.'

Bean rubbed his palm along his left thigh; a sure sign that he'd reached his decision. 'I think you're both crazy,' he said. 'Crazy and wrong. But you are my best friends and therefore I'm obliged to say, Jack, any dead friends of yours are dead friends of mine.'

'So, you're in?'

'I'm in. On one condition.'

'Which is?'

'That you accept that a team of three isn't sufficient. We need to get some more people on board.'

'To be honest, I didn't expect either of you to say yes,'

I admitted. 'And I mean this with the greatest respect - who else is mad enough?'

'I think there are three people who would jump at the chance.' Bean's face lit up for the first time since our conversation began.

13.

We found Wee Drop standing outside the bookies, staring in.

'Used t'be wee drop bake,' he said.

'It hasn't been a bakery for over ten years,' Stew said.

Wee Drop looked down the length of the street. 'Now only wee drop fam.'

'You're right,' I said. 'Family businesses used to be at the heart of our community. Now it's nearly all corporates and charity shops.'

Wee Drop nodded sadly.

I pushed on, grateful for the opening. 'You can't have community unless people know and trust each other,' I said. 'Unless they are willing to work together.'

'In a committed team,' Bean said.

'With everyone willing to do the right thing,' Stew added.

'No matter what it takes,' I said.

Wee Drop looked at us one-at-a-time. He considered briefly and then took a step forward. We all moved back instinctively. Suddenly we had returned to the playground and the teacher was asserting his authority. The boys who had been feeling smart and smug just a few seconds ago, were now shuffling in place like a chain gang that had lost its rhythm.

'Need a wee drop expla,' the teacher said, dropping his inflexion in the commanding, seen-it-all-before manner of an experienced Sergeant Major.

The three of us glanced at each other. As Wee Drop had been the first on Bean's list of possible teammates, I thought he should speak. Bean made it clear the responsibility was all mine.

'I'd be pleased to explain,' I said, aware that my best friends were trying to subtly distance themselves from me. 'There is, though, quite a lot of explaining to do, so it might be better if we find somewhere to sit down?'

We went back to the pub.

The place was still empty. Morgan didn't look surprised to see us. We sat at our usual table.

When the drinks arrived, I told Wee Drop everything. He remained silent throughout. He didn't show the slightest element of surprise. He might as well have been listening to a pupil reciting a well-known story.

'And that's it,' I said, when there was nothing more to reveal. 'That's everything. That's where we were, where we are now, how we got here, and what we're planning to do about it. Bean thought -' My friend glared. '- I mean, we all thought, that you'd be a great addition to the team. What do you say?'

Wee Drop reached across the table and patted the back of my hand briefly. 'You need more than wee drop hel,' he said. 'And I'll def add more than wee drop val.'

'You're right, we do need help.'

Wee Drop looked at me and saw the rest of the bar at the same time.

Only the best teachers could do that. They were the ones I never messed with. They'd be kneeling by your desk, seemingly giving you all their attention and then, without looking away even for a split-second, they'd click their fingers at Damien Jones, who'd dropped his pencil on the floor and was trying to look up Sally Smith's skirt.

At that moment, as Wee Drop looked at me, I was prepared to believe that he had eyes in the back of his head. Which, on its own, would be an excellent reason for having him in the team.

'So, can we count on you?'

Wee Drop tapped his foot against the grubby wooden floor. He considered for a moment, then he reached out to shake my hand.

14.

I left the three of them in The Frog & Bull about to engage in, what Stew insisted would be, a period of team building. Bean had convinced me that I should approach the other two intended team members on my own. At this time of day, they would both be in the same building. If I timed it right, I'd catch them together.

It took me twenty minutes to reach the Daisy Street Baths. It was the oldest swimming pool in the county, dating back to Victorian times. During the 1918 Spanish Flu pandemic, when several thousand people had died in the city in just one month, the building had been used to store their bodies. Now, thanks to a generous donation from an unknown benefactor, it was still functioning as a leisure centre with a fifty-metre indoor pool.

Like other leisure centres, it had re-opened a couple of months ago and, although people were still Covid-cautious, they were beginning to return.

I paid my entrance fee, went up to the viewing gallery and looked down into the pool.

The Paddington Fish was precisely where I expected him to be. He was in the deep end, sitting cross-legged on the bottom of the pool. Above him, half-a-dozen swimmers crawled, breast- or back-stroked their way through the water. I was there for just over four minutes before he allowed himself to float slowly up to the surface. When his face broke water, he turned a calm three-sixty, inhaled once, and returned to the bottom. For the next half-an-hour, the swimmers continued their rigorous journeys, going nowhere.

The Fish popped up half-a-dozen times, circled once, and submerged with minimum fuss. When he finally left the water, he was in and out of the changing rooms in the time it took me to get down from the gallery.

I caught up with him in the reception area. His handshake was smooth and flat, more a slip-in-and-slide-out than a grip.

'How's life below the surface?'

'Pressured.' The Fish blinked a couple of times. 'And quiet.'

He'd worked as a diver on oil rigs for the best part of 20 years. The story was that he'd saved a lot of money. Now he spent a couple of hours every day just sitting on the bottom of the Daisy Street swimming pool whilst others counted their lengths above him. It had taken a while for people – swimmers and leisure centre staff - to accept that he wasn't a pervert with an unusual lung capacity. Now, though, the regulars barely noticed his presence.

The Fish had welcomed that. I guess professional deep-sea divers are happy with their own company. The Fish certainly was. I hoped that, just this once, he'd be willing to a work cooperatively in a team.

'Quiet is good,' I said, hoping my voice wasn't too loud. 'Too many people make too much noise, and most of it isn't worth listening to. In fact, some of it's downright harmful.'

The Fish blinked.

'So, er, have you thought at all about that brilliant idea

I came up with a couple of months ago?'

He shook his head.

'I think you should. With a bit of help from the right individuals, you could become a social media superstar. All it would take are some films of you sitting there, underwater, holding your breath for ages. And on the back of that you could talk about how good it is for your physical and mental health, and then you could do some instructional films, showing people how they could submerge themselves in their bath, or put their head in the sink, and do a form of breath-holding, underwater meditation.

'I reckon you could relate it to being in the womb. Maybe do a special course for pregnant women, explaining how it will make them develop an even closer connection with their baby. And one for people with tinnitus, pointing out that fish never have problems with their ears. And one for people who too-often experience a sinking feeling. You could help them reframe it into something positive. In fact, I'd probably sign up for that myself. And then there are those who are bored doing yoga and mindfulness and are looking for the next big thing.

'All you need is one major celebrity to follow your training and give you a testimonial and, before you know it, you'll be a cult figure known across the world. If you could teach people how to stay cool in hot water that would be the icing on the cake. In a manner of speaking.'

'I like to be off Grid,' the Fish said softly. 'And I don't make plans.'

'Of course. You prefer to go with the flow.' I appreciated how stupid that line was about two seconds too late.

The Fish just looked at me. I checked his chest, to make sure that he was breathing. It was hard to tell.

107

'Actually, I haven't come to see you about the social media idea,' I said. 'It's about something much more important. There's something terrible happening. I need to stop it, and I really need your help.'

Not one part of the Fish's face moved. His body was completely still. He remained silent. I reminded myself that deep sea creatures were not famous for their blatant displays of emotion.

I decided to cut to the chase.

'Ok. So, er, the thing is, and I know this is coming out of left field, there's a p-n-j wreaking havoc – and I mean really awful, terrible, havoc, not just run-of-the-mill havoc – and I have to catch him. And I need all the help I can get.'

'A psycho-nut-job?' The Fish pursed his lips. 'You're going after a genuine psycho-nut-job?'

'Yes.' I did a quick double-take. 'How did you know that a p-n-j is a psycho-nut-job? I didn't mean to say p-n-j, I meant to say psycho-nut-job, but sometimes I abbreviate just to save time and sometimes because I'm feeling stressed, and...' My voice trailed off. A part of my mind suggested throwing some more abbreviations his way to see if this was another superpower he possessed.

Before I could decide what to say, Thoughtless walked into the reception area.

15.

'Jack! I haven't seen you in a while.' The smile of greeting was warm and fluid. 'If you'd got here an hour earlier, you could have joined my class.'

Thoughtless taught yoga and mindfulness and wasn't looking for the next big thing. Thoughtless spent 3 months of every year in India, studying under the sort of high-level

Gurus that you only met if you were a super-dedicated practitioner who was in the know.

Thoughtless made yoga look easy. I tried it once and discovered it wasn't.

Thoughtless had a handshake that was the firm, confident and welcoming opposite of what the Fish offered.

'I'm going to leave yoga to those people with more muscle power, physical control and self-assurance, than me,' I said, trying to look rueful.

'Yoga meets individuals at their own starting point,' Thoughtless replied. 'You don't need to possess any special attributes to practise. You just have to step on the path.'

'And then be willing to keep moving?'

'Of course.'

'You see, there's my problem.' I smiled. 'That requires too much effort. I don't want a path I have to follow; I want an escalator to take me.'

'I'm afraid there isn't a yoga escalator,' Thoughtless chuckled. 'That would defeat the purpose.'

'You've got a Downward Dog and an Extended Puppy; I don't see why you can't have an Escalator.'

Thoughtless put a strong hand on my shoulder and squeezed gently. 'The classes will always be here if you ever change your mind.'

'Thanks.'

'Remember, we're all capable of changing direction.'

'Well, in once sense I have. That's why I came here to see you both.' I glanced at the Fish. 'I was just explaining my situation when you joined us.' I cleared my throat. 'How do you feel about joining an elite team, formed with the specific purpose of hunting down a maniacal killer?'

'A psycho-nut-job,' the Fish whispered.

Thoughtless frowned. I was struck by the fact that somehow even that looked healthy and peaceful. 'Sorry, I appreciate the offer – genuinely, I do – but I don't play computer games.'

'This isn't a computer game. There's a real guy targeting real prostitutes.'

'I didn't know,' Thoughtless said. 'I don't read newspapers or watch the news.'

'It wouldn't matter if you did, it's barely had a mention. That's why I've promised to catch him.'

'Who have you made that promise to?'

'Ah, now...' I looked from Thoughtless to the Fish and back again, '...That's the thing that makes all of this a bit unusual.'

'That's the thing?' Thoughtless smiled again. The Fish stepped closer, his mouth open.

'Yeah. Well, statistically, it's very unusual. However, depending on your worldview, it might be quite acceptable. You know, it's all a question of what you believe and what you don't believe, and what you've experienced and what you've never experienced. It's more a matter of where you're at with the ultimate nature of things, beginnings and endings, and levels of reality, than it is about the everyday stuff we just take for granted. If that makes sense.'

'It doesn't,' the Fish said, although his mouth barely moved.

'To be fair, it didn't to me, and I said it.' I licked my lips, trying to create some moisture that I could use to shape better words.

'Just make the honest sounds,' Thoughtless said. 'Let them come from your heart, rather than your mouth. When you speak from the heart, other people automatically feel it in theirs. Just forget yourself and be the vehicle for honest sounds.'

Even the Fish raised an eyebrow when he heard that.

'Right. Ok.' I swallowed. I tried to say something, but my mouth felt empty. I told myself to just make honest sounds, but my throat refused to cooperate. 'It's hard to know what to let go of,' I said. 'It feels like there's stuff in the way.'

'The body holds onto things,' Thoughtless said. 'Over time, all the little things it holds onto build into blockages. That's the downside of social conditioning. That's the price we pay for creating cultures. We lose who we really are, because we are too busy trying to conform, or trying to be different. Either way, we learn to instinctively cling onto so much of what comes our way, or what happened in the past. That isn't our true nature, though. We are processing beings, not storage facilities.'

I felt my self-storage unit nodding, although I'd no idea why. I felt blocked, both physically and mentally.

'Let's walk and talk,' Thoughtless said. 'When the mind gets stuck, it's always a good idea to move the body. We'll go through the Arboretum, and let the trees inspire us.'

16.

I don't know if the trees made any difference, but a path lined with Lavvies really helped. The pond with a large fountain at its centre seemed to work well for the Fish, too.

By the time we'd done a couple of circuits, I'd told them my story in full. It hadn't become any easier. In the silence that followed, Thoughtless performed a stretch that involved both hands reaching up towards the sky and then coming down to touch the earth. The Fish stared at the fountain.

'You're going into deep water,' he said, finally. 'And deep water's no place for amateurs.'

'That's why I'm asking you,' I said.

'I dived into the real stuff, not the metaphor.'

'Precisely. You're used to pressure. Risk management is something you take for granted. Attention to detail is second nature to someone like you. Bean, Stew and I only ever give attention to possible quiz answers, and the most pressure we've felt, before this, was dealing with an RSPCA Inspector.'

'You, too?' Thoughtless stopped exercising. 'You've also had a visit?'

'Well, not me, not directly. But he helped tip one of the Shades over the edge, whilst he was still alive obviously, and he accused Bean of tying up a snake.'

'He's really doing the rounds,' Thoughtless did the peaceful frown. 'He came knocking on my door a couple of weeks ago. He said he'd received a report that I'd been forcing a rabbit into inappropriate poses. I said that I didn't own any rabbits, but he insisted on looking around. Then I realised the reason for his confusion. I told him that, although I didn't have a pet rabbit, I did practise the rabbit pose. It's called sasangasana. It's great for connecting with nature. It brings out the gentle playfulness of bunnies. When I started showing him, he was out of the door like a shot. Left his card, though.'

'And his visit didn't bother you? You didn't find it weird?'

'I figure he's misinformed and trying to find his place, just like the rest of us.'

'The Shades are still trying to find their place, too,' I said. 'They're still on the path – a different path to us. Or, at least, if it's the same path, they're much further along it, and they're all desperate to know where to go next. To be honest with you, I don't think they'll be going anywhere until the killer is brought to justice. That's the point. I'm not really asking you to help me. I'm asking you to help the

Shades. I'm asking you to help them move on.'

'You've always got to keep moving,' the Fish said.

Which struck me as counter-intuitive, coming from a man who spent so much time sitting still in the deep-end.

'You're right,' Thoughtless replied. 'Movement is the most basic principle of life. It's what connects all of nature.'

My instinct was to ask why, if you're born human, you'd want to move like a bunny, but then it struck me that I probably don't know what it means to truly move like a human, so I binned that avenue of enquiry.

'Do you believe we ever stop moving?' I asked them both.

'Never,' they replied as one.

'It's just that some movements are more subtle than others,' Thoughtless added.

'I would have expected Shades to understand that better than we do,' the Fish said. 'After all, they've had more experience.'

I shook my head. 'The experience they had when they passed wasn't subtle. In fact, the way they talk about it, the first stage of dying is the opposite of subtle.'

The Fish looked over at the fountain. 'Being on the ocean bed,' he began, 'is like being in a different world. It changes your perspective because you leave behind everything that you take for granted. You learn through direct experience that your life is just one incredibly tiny, interconnected, part of the great complexity of everything.'

'I'm with you on the complexity thing,' I said, offering my best impression of a wise sage.[18]

The Fish carried on as if I hadn't spoken. 'The sad thing

---

[18] It's not my best impression. (Not as bad as my Kevin McCloud, though.)

is that, despite working for years underwater, in the most foreign of places, it's still impossible to avoid making assumptions. I still assumed how the Shades would be.'

'It's part of the human condition,' Thoughtless said. 'I don't think it's something we can ever be fully free from. And based on what Jack's just told us, we're not even free from it in the first stages of the life after this.'

'I'll tell you something I've always assumed,' I said, taking the opportunity to bond even more with the Fish. 'That fish can't feel anything, and that's why it's Ok to go fishing.'

'Have you ever been fishing?' The Fish kept his eyes on the fountain.

'No.'

'Why not?'

'I'm uncomfortable around water.'

'Over seventy percent of the planet is covered in water,' the Fish said. 'Plus, there's water in the air, in the soil, and inside every human being.'

'That would explain why I'm always uncomfortable.'

The Fish swallowed. 'Life began in the oceans,' he said. 'That's where we came from. It was our original home. We should remember that. And just because fish have faces that tend to lack expression, it's a mistake to think they don't feel pain and, even, emotion. They have nervous systems that ensure they do.'

'Do you spend so much time sitting on the bottom of the pool because you miss working in the ocean?'

'No.'

'Then why do you do it?'

'Why do mountaineers climb mountains?'

'Because they are there?'

'It's got nothing to do with the mountains.'

In my peripheral vision, I saw Thoughtless smiling.

Once again, I was the only one in the class who didn't know the right answer. It was time to stop trying to bond with the Fish and ask the question that mattered most.

'Are you going to join the team?'

'Yes.' For the second time, they spoke together.

A wave of relief flooded my system. It was followed instantly by the silent question,

'How are these two going to get on with the other three?'

My brain conjured up a mental film of Bean Curry, Stew Gardner, Wee Drop, the Paddington Fish and Thoughtless sitting round a table trying to come up with a plan to catch a p-n-j. The film was in black and white. It was like something from the 1930's.

An overwhelmingly negative assumption rattled down my vagus nerve like a bowling ball hurtling down the centre of a lane. It hit my stomach full force, driving all before it.

Strike!

Morgan

1.

'Reality exists in the space between two people.'
Epiah Khan

'It felt like my stomach was going to explode,' I told Bean and Stew when I finally caught up with them in the pub. 'Talk about a powerful gut feeling.'

'The gut is connected to the brain via the heart and the vagus nerve,' Bean said. 'It's directly affected by our emotional state and the degree of stress we are experiencing.'

'We house many, many trillions of bugs in our gut,' Stew added, keen not to be outdone on the topic. 'In recent years, scientists have become increasingly aware of the importance of gut health in relation to our overall wellbeing.'

'Knowledge we three are aware of yet choose not to act upon.' Bean raised his glass solemnly. It was only late afternoon, but he was on the Cabernet already. 'To stubborn refusal.'

'To stubborn refusal.'

We clinked glasses and reflected silently as we drank.

I gave us all a few seconds, before moving us on. 'Right, back to business,' I rapped the tabletop with my knuckles. 'How did things go with Wee Drop?'

'Good as could be expected,' Stew said. 'He didn't stay too long, and he didn't say too much, but he's coming back tonight and he's definitely up for it. How about the other two?'

'They'll be here at seven.'

'Then we have a team, and that means we'll need a team leader.' Stew looked pointedly at Bean.

He shook his head.

'We don't have a team, not yet,' he said. 'All we've got right now is a collection of individuals, who some might regard as a motley crew.'

'A heavy metal band,' Stew said. 'Formed by Nikki Sixx, Tommy Lee, Vince Neil and, erm...'

'Mick Mars on lead guitar,' I finished it before Stew could. 'They came together in Los Angeles in 1981. The interesting thing about the band's name -'

' – Is how they came up with it.' Bean cut me off. 'Mick Mars had once been in a band that had been described as a motley crew. The others liked that, so they changed the spelling of *crew* and added the umlauts over the *o* and the *u*.'

'This is mine to finish,' Stew was in the instant Bean paused for breath. 'They got the idea for the umlauts from the beer they preferred at the time, which was Löwenbräu.'

'Umlauts were popular with other heavy metal bands at that time,' Bean wouldn't be stopped. 'They used them to show boldness and strength. Motörhead, is arguably the most famous example.'

'Well,' I said, 'it's good to see that this actual team within our motley crew, is in fine working order. If we were quizzing tonight, we'd be unbeatable.'

'We're pretty much unbeatable any night,' Stew said.

'The question is, can we be unbeatable when we're not quizzing?' Bean leant in as he spoke. 'That's the question that really matters.'

I stood up. 'You're right. Nothing's ever mattered as much.'

'I'll drink to that.' Stew raised his glass. It was empty. He pretended that he hadn't seen. I dropped a tenner on the table.

'The next round's on me. Buy yourself a pint and get Bean another bottle. I think we've got a long night ahead.'

'You don't want one?'

'No. I need to nip back to 5a. I've got a question of my own that I need an answer to.'

2.

It felt like I'd been away from the Shades for a long time, so I walked faster than I normally would, using that ridiculous pace that's quicker than a stroll but too slow to be a jog.

As I neared home, a white van passed me. The driver beeped and, as I waved instinctively, he flashed me the V sign. I didn't respond. Sometimes questions take up all our energy and fill up all our space. Sometimes questions are so big nothing else can get through. I was wrapped up in one of those right now. I felt like I was suffocating.

When I opened the front door, the Shades were waiting for me. They were wrapped up in a question of their own.

Bella got straight down to it. 'Have you got a team?'

'Yes.' I wanted to sit down, but my adrenaline wouldn't let me. 'Everyone I asked agreed to help.'

'Jeez...' Bella took a moment to look at Doreen and Darius. If they'd been able to do a group hug, they would have. 'So, it's really happening, you're really doing this for us?'

'I said I would.'

'Yeah.'

Bella saw my fatigue and stress.

'Share with me, sweetheart. Tell me about it.' Her voice was suddenly the softest thing known to man. I couldn't help but tell her about it.

'I'm not used to revealing myself,' I said. 'I've known these men for years and today I've admitted to them that, for all the time we've been mates, I've been lying by omission, I've kept secret the most important thing there is to know about me. It's like, by telling them now, because I need something from them, I'm saying that I didn't trust them with it before.'

'Or you didn't trust yourself before? Maybe it was that, hey?'

I swear I felt Bella's voice soothe my brow. I kept talking.

'It's so hard when there are words that you've known for years – forever – words about yourself that you've never had to say before. It's so hard to let them out of your mouth. Once they're gone, you can't get them back, and you've no idea what other people will do with them. It's like you're really showing someone who you are, and you're hoping - not trusting, you're a long way from trusting – you're hoping that they'll be Ok with it.'

'And they all were?'

'Yes.'

'Then they proved to you that they're real friends. You can't ask for any more than that. The world's filled with people who don't have any real friends.'

'I know.'

'You should be feeling grateful.'

'I am.'

'Then why have you got that look on your face? The look you have when there's something you need to ask, but you're scared of what the answer might be. What is it?'

'It's, erm...it's a thing that's never crossed my mind until recently.' I collapsed into my chair and looked up into my Shade-sister's eyes. I would have given anything to have seen my reflection in her delicate, light-blue orbs.

'You don't need to be scared,' she said.

'I can't help it,' I said.

'Ask it anyway,' she said.

I closed my eyes and tried to hide in the darkness.

My mouth asked, 'Are you real?'

3.

I felt, rather than saw, Bella begin to pace. I opened my eyes. I feared there would be anger on her face, but there wasn't. For the first time ever, it looked like she was struggling to find the right words. Doreen and Darius were watching her intently. We all waited.

Finally, Bella said, 'I have no idea.'

It wasn't the answer I was hoping for.

'Why not?'

'Because I don't do – can't do – any of the things that I used to. I can't physically feel me, let alone anyone. All that seems to have happened is that I've lost most of me, and I've got nothing new. It's more like I'm disappearing, rather than changing.' She paused, considered briefly, and said, 'The best answer I've got to your question, is that we're as real as everything else you can see or talk to. And so was your grandpa when he spoke to you at his funeral. He was as real then as he ever had been before. Does that help?'

'I've got to make sure it does.'

Bella looked at me closely. 'Why did you ask?'

'Because of something that was said, because of things I heard myself say.'

'And?'

'I started wondering if you were really here or not. You know, whether I'm a real psychic medium and my relationships with you are true. Or if I've been living in the

120

Black Hole for years without recognising it.'

'You mean, if we're only in your imagination and you never knew?'

'Yeah.' I nodded. 'I really need you to be here. I don't know how I can carry on if you're not. I need to be sure I'm not talking into space, that I haven't just proved to everyone I know that I belong in the loony bin.'

'I get that.'

'So, help me know for sure.'

'I can't. I've got no idea how to. In the end, though, it's not me you need to listen to.'

'Then who?'

'It's not who, it's what.' Bella pointed at my chest. 'What does your heart tell you?'

'For some reason, today everyone's talking about hearts.'

'Well?'

I considered.

It was one of the few moments in my life, apart from those times swirling around the edges of the Black Hole, that I'd ever been aware of my heart doing its thing. It was thudding like a heavy fist against an even heavier door. I was sure I heard it scream into the tempest of my fear. I felt my stomach tense and churn. Then I found I could breathe again.

'It tells me you're as real as everything else I can see or talk to,' I said, 'and that you're the only ones I'd put myself through this for.'

'There we are, then.' I'd never seen Bella look so pleased with herself. 'So what happens next?'

'We're going to have our first team meeting,' I said. 'Actually, that's not right. It's not a team meeting.' I straightened in my chair. 'It's a war council.'

4.

I left 5a just after 6pm. I wanted to be at the pub early.

Morgan was on the Boulevard, heading in the same direction. I made a point of catching her up.

'Guten.'

'Guten'

'Abend.'

'Abend.'

'Morgan.'

'Morgan.'

Somethings make you smile no matter how many times you do them. We both smiled. I waited a couple of paces before saying, 'How are you doing now?'

'What do you mean *now*?' She didn't change her step.

'It's eleven weeks and three days since you broke off your engagement with Thaddeus.'

'Eleven weeks and three days exactly.'

'That was a lucky guess, then.' I coughed.

'Was it?' Morgan glanced at me and smiled.

'I haven't been counting.'

'Would you tell me if you had?'

I looked up at the sky. Even the moon was hiding. I could hear Bella saying, 'You're on your own with this.'

And she was right. Not only was I on my own, I deserved to be. Sometimes, I guess, you have to be on your own to accept that something is true.

Sometimes we have such a day. Sometimes we have a day that frees us if we let it. I was having one now. I'd swum so far into the ocean, there was no point turning back.

'Yes,' I said, ignoring my feet by doing the opposite and looking up into the sky. 'I would tell you.'

'And?'

I breathed deeply. 'Of course I was counting.'

'Wow.'

'Wow, what exactly?'

'Wow, I was hoping you were.'

'Oh.'

I realised I was now looking down at my feet. I glanced across at Morgan. She was looking at hers, too.

We watched ourselves walk. It was clear that I needed to take the lead.

I said, 'You never actually told me why.'

'Why what?'

'Why you broke off the engagement. You were planning your wedding and you stopped it dead.'

'Have you ever wanted to share your life with someone?' Morgan slowed her pace as she asked the question, adjusting her movement to the tempo and tone of her words.

It's something I've noticed that women are naturally good at. It's like they've had lessons that all the boys missed.

It seems to me that women know how to be congruent, even when they're faking it. Men are just a collection of parts, all going in different directions and giving different messages simultaneously. Men are difficult to understand, but it's not because we're deep and mysterious. We're difficult to understand because we're literally all over the place, disjointed and confused, trying to behave in all the different ways we believe men should.

'Well?' Morgan pushed the question. 'Have you ever wanted to?'

I thought of Bella. I looked at Morgan.

'My parents were together for just over fifty years,' I said. 'They shared their lives, but they didn't share their love – not throughout it all. I don't know when they stopped truly loving each other, but it happened decades before they died.'

'That's so sad.'

'There are worse things.'

'Sharing your life with someone shouldn't just be a habit. It should be much more than that. It should be magical.'

The courage needed to take the lead threatened to slip away. 'If magic is needed, then I wouldn't recommend me to anyone.'

Morgan stopped walking. She placed her hand on my forearm. 'Stop being so harsh with yourself.'

'Trust me on this, there's a very good chance that, as a magical life partner, I'd be more Tommy Cooper than David Copperfield.'

'Thomas Frederick Cooper was a genius,' Morgan smiled. I felt her fingers squeeze my arm gently. 'He was a master magician and a member of The Magic Circle, an organisation dedicated to advancing and promoting the art of magic. Only the very best magicians ever qualify for membership. So, if you'd be as great a partner as Tommy Cooper was a magician, any girl would be lucky to have you.'

'I'd temporarily forgotten that you wrote all the questions.'

'Which means I know all the answers.'

'So why did you break off the engagement?'

Morgan took her hand away. 'Sometimes you just have to trust your instinct,' she said finally. 'Sometimes, even when everything looks right, you must allow yourself to be guided by your sense of the unseen. When you feel there's some invisible force trying to guide you, you have to let it. I think there's more to life – more to us – than just the obvious stuff.' She forced a smile. 'Does that sound silly?'

I imagined Bella, leaning with her arm on Doreen's

shoulder and one eyebrow raised, as she waited for my reply. I knew that, at the very least, the teacher in her would send me to the naughty corner if I said the wrong thing.

'It doesn't sound even remotely silly,' I said. 'In fact, I couldn't agree with you more. There's far more to life than most people see.'

Morgan's hand returned to my arm. 'I think that being true partners means sharing the invisible things as well as all the rest. And I think that true love – the sort that never gets taken over by habit - is an undeniable force that makes you look at everything differently.'

In my imagination, Bella and Doreen both straightened, silently imploring me to say something obvious like, 'I think that's something we should talk about over a few drinks.' But just when I didn't need it to, my mouth offered its usual form of distraction.

'I'm more inclined to think that, over time, true love deafens you,' I heard it say. 'It deafens you to the different sounds your partner makes as they age. When you're young all you hear is the magical rhythm of their voice, their groans and yells of pleasure, the softness of their breathing as they sleep next to you. Fast forward four decades and the only groaning you hear is as they get out of a chair. When they're eating food, they sound like a washing machine slowly breaking down. When they sleep, they throw out the sort of machine gun noises that kids make when they're running around in the playground. True love stops you hearing all that - true love, and the inevitable build-up of car wax.'

Morgan's smile somehow managed to combine humour with curiosity and more than a soupcon of irritation.

'Why did you turn to that?' She asked.

'Turn to what?'

'Humour.'

'Thanks for recognising it.'

'Answer, please.'

The most important thing I learnt at school was that making people smile stops them from picking on you. It helps you hide in plain sight. At best, you become known as the school comedian. At worst, as the boy who's not always as funny as he thinks he is. Either way, you've created a label that doesn't read *Victim*.

Nowadays, for me, the role of joke-writer has combined with that of Celebrant, to offer twin layers of protection. They work like an invisible bullet-proof vest, or like Clark Kent's Superman outfit hidden underneath his suit. The problem is, neither offer a 100% guarantee of safety. A hand grenade blows you and the vest into a thousand bits. Kryptonite does away with Superman. The Black Hole doesn't do funny. And it adores grief.

I've always really liked Morgan. Actually, I've always more than liked her. So much so, that I wanted to be honest with her. I mean, Black Hole and Shades honest. I just hadn't caught up with her tonight expecting the possibility of such a heart-to-heart. I'd been expecting more of a gossip than a reveal.

Now I knew that if I didn't answer her question honestly, the chance of Black Hole and Shade honesty might be lost forever. I took another deep breath.

'The reason I turned to humour,' I said, 'Is because it's a defensive habit. It's one that I developed a long time ago.'

'Why do you have to be defensive with me?' Her hand was soft and reassuring.

'Because it limits the risk of pain.'

'I would never hurt you deliberately.'

'Isn't that what makes it worse?'

Morgan remained silent, just watching me. Women are

terrifyingly good at that, too.

My mouth managed, 'I really need you to give me a reason to talk.'

Morgan nodded. 'Why do you write puns instead of longer routines? What's the real reason?'

My mouth seemed surprisingly keen to respond to that. 'The, erm, the first part of the reason is that puns are obviously much shorter.'

'Are you saying that makes them easier to write?'

'No. Not at all. The issue isn't about the process of creating them, it's about how they're received.'

'What do you mean?'

'I don't sell every joke that I offer. Quite a few are rejected. I find it easier to deal with having a dozen one-line puns turned down, than I would a much bigger piece of material.'

'Even though they've still taken a lot of work?'

'Yes.'

'Ok. What's the second part of the reason?'

'Puns are silly, or they rely on some clever wordplay. You're not really commenting on anything. You're not out there, giving your take on the world.'

'You wouldn't want to do that?'

'No.'

'But you're out there with Bean and Stew when you're quizzing?'

'That's not the same thing. All we're doing then is showing off how many ultimately irrelevant facts we know. The only thing you discover about us, is that we don't have many friends and spend far too much time trawling for information. As a quizzer, I'm not giving you my view on different things, I'm just demonstrating that I've got a great memory. And that I like to win.'

'Maybe you should start pushing at your boundaries a

little bit? Maybe, for example, you could write yourself a short routine made up of a series of puns about a common topic? Maybe you could begin doing your own stand-up? That might be a good starting point.'

'No. I think I'm too old for that.'

'No, you're not.'

'Trust me. I might not look it on the outside, but inside I'm much older than my years.'

'What on earth makes you think that?'

'The noises I make when I get out of a chair.'

5.

When we reached The Frog & Bull, Morgan went upstairs. She paused halfway, glanced over her shoulder, and smiled at me. We had exchanged our mobile phone numbers. I had promised to write and perform a brief comedy set. I hadn't said where or when. We had agreed to have a few drinks together. We hadn't agreed where or when. I needed to catch a killer first. Only I couldn't tell her that. There were other things I had to share first.

I headed into the bar.

Everyone was already there. Someone had put two rectangular tables together. Bean and Stew were sitting one on side. Wee Drop, the Paddington Fish and Thoughtless were on the other. I sat in the empty chair to Bean's right.

'Pity there isn't a large, round table we could have used.'

'That wouldn't have made you Arthur,' Bean said. 'If we were suddenly transported into the legend of Camelot, you'd have a very different role.'

'Which would be?'

'Court Jester.'

It was hard to argue with that.

'And, given how much time you've spent in hospital,' Stew slapped Bean on the shoulder. 'You'd have been Lanced-a-lot.'

No one laughed. Bean made a point of yawning. 'And you'd have been Bors the Younger.' He nodded towards Morgan as she appeared briefly behind the bar. 'At least we'd have had our own ready-made Morgan le Fay.'

'Good call.' Stew jumped back into the security of quizzing trivia. 'Morgan the Fairy, the powerful enchantress of the Arthurian legend. According to the stories, she began as Arthur's benevolent protector, but over time she became an antagonist whose moral compass could turn in any direction.'

For some reason, that description made me shiver.

'Here's a question for you,' Thoughtless leant forwards. 'Is an expert quizzer actually an expert, or are they just a brilliant jack of all trades?'

'Fairly obviously, if the quizzer is me, then he's a Jack of all trades.' I tipped my head in a brief bow to the others and took my first drink of the night. It looked like Bean and Stew had been here all day.

'We're experts,' Stew said firmly. 'We're experts because we know far more than the usual guy in the street, and because we know how to apply our knowledge under pressure.'

'But you're not experts in the same way that, say, a surgeon is,' Thoughtless said. 'You haven't delved deeply into one area of study.'

'Let's keep the medical profession out of this,' Bean scratched his leg and shuffled in his seat.

'One of the biggest problems in the world today,' Stew said, 'is that everyone thinks they're an expert. They think they have the right to make decisions about topics they barely understand.

'This was started by those TV talent shows that let the home audience, rather than experts, decide the overall winner. Now we have people sitting at home, telling it like it is to the television screen. Now everyone believes they know everything, and all opinions are equally valid.

'That's what enabled Michael Gove, when he was busy persuading people to vote for Brexit, to say that people in this country have had enough of experts. The self-serving moron! You're only indifferent to expertise until you need it to save you. If I was in charge of the country, I'd run a poll asking who'd had enough of experts. Everyone who said they had, would be forced by law to do everything for themselves, from fixing their car to doing their own rewiring and plumbing, from taking out their own teeth to creating their own medicines. From heart surgery to -'

'- Ok Stew, we get the point.' Bean stopped what was in danger of becoming a twenty-minute tirade.

'Sorry,' Thoughtless looked more than a little sheepish. 'I was just curious.'

'Curiosity is king,' I said.

'Indeed, it is,' Bean confirmed. 'So, let's get curious, can we, about the topic at hand. Jack, how do you want us to go at this?'

The moment I hadn't been looking forward to suddenly leaped out and put its arms around my chest. And I was more ready for it than I had expected. I started talking.

'Guys, I'm going to be honest with you,' I said. 'I'm not a planner. I don't have the faintest clue how to go about this. I don't just need you to help me do it, I need your help working out what to do in the first place. And I mean that literally. I don't even know how we should begin this. I need one of you to tell me.'

No one spoke. No one moved. No one even blinked. Suddenly, it was so quiet around our table you'd have thought we weren't there.

Eventually, Wee Drop said, 'Wee drop prob. Only wee drop. No big d.'

It was the most reassuring thing I could have heard.

'Thanks. I was bothered that I might have put you all off.'

'Of course not,' Bean took over. 'We just need a mechanism for warming up, for getting our minds going the way we do before a quiz.'

'How do you do that?' Thoughtless asked.

'We have different ways,' Stew said.

'But the best way, by far,' Bean's face reddened as it did every time he dredged up the answer to a seemingly impossible question. 'The absolutely best way, is to play a round of Sad Puddings.'

6.

I should have thought of it. Rather than backing away from the unknown and relying on someone else to step forward, I should have asked myself the question, what do I know that I can use?

Message to self: It's not enough to take your hands out of your pockets and to stop looking at your shoes; you've also got to take the initiative.

'Actions speak louder than words.'

Everyone looked at me.

'Sorry. Didn't mean to say that out loud.'

'Jus wee drop slip,' Wee Drop instinctively told the class not to make a big deal out of it.

'You're right,' I said. 'Just a little slippage between mind and mouth. Apologies. It won't happen again.'

'Good to know.' Bean turned to Stew. 'Do you have the cards?'

'Never without them.'

'Then we're in business.'

Stew addressed the Sad Pudding virgins in his Master of the Cards voice. 'I have here a deck of homemade cards, each with a specific game attached to it.' He removed the deck from his pocket and placed it on the table. 'I spread them out face-down like this and pick one at random. Whatever game is on the card is the game we play. Is that clear?'

'What if you pick a game that's of no use to us?' The Paddington Fish asked the question without sounding concerned or condemnatory.

I should have prioritised answering him, but instead I looked to see if he was holding his breath. Consequently, Bean got there before me.

'There's no chance of that happening,' he said. 'They're all good. Whatever game it is, it will help us.'

'Are they like Tarot cards?' Thoughtless asked.

'Nothing like. Sad Puddings gets your neurons firing. It gets your brain sparky. It makes you think faster.'

'Why is it called Sad Puddings?'

'Don't ask.' I got in on that one. As far as I could tell, the Paddington Fish was breathing only slightly more frequently than a corpse.

'Right,' Stew placed his left hand over the cards. 'Let's get on with it.' He made as if to select a card from the centre of the pack, and then changed his mind. 'We'll have you,' he said, turning over one from the end of the line.

It was FoF. One of Stew's favourite games. The card had nothing on it but the three letters.

'Wee drop ab,' Wee Drop observed.

'It is, indeed,' Bean said. 'It's an abbreviation for *Fact or Fiction*. Essentially, Stew, as the Master of the Cards, will tell us something. Our job is to decide if it's a fact, in which case we need to say something about it – in this case, we'll explore how, or if, it can help us to catch a killer. If it's not a fact we have to dismiss it in the most interesting, original, or abusive way possible.'

To their eternal credit none of the Sad Pudding virgins looked even remotely surprised or confused.

'It's a team game,' Stew said. 'You are allowed – indeed, encouraged – to collaborate and share knowledge and ideas. However, you have only 2 minutes to decide whether what I say is fact or fiction. After that, you have as much time as you like to either talk about the fact or be creatively dismissive with the fiction. If you come to the wrong conclusion and dismiss a fact or, alternatively, mistakenly factualise fiction, I win. If you get it right, you win. It's that straightforward. Ready?'

'Never been readier.' I spoke on behalf of the team.

Bean tipped his head slightly to one side and rested both hands on his ample stomach in his usual quizzing posture. Thoughtless brought both legs up onto the chair and assumed a full lotus posture. If any other human being had done that, it would have looked more than a little self-promoting. Thoughtless, however, made it look like the most natural thing in the world. The Paddington Fish inhaled slow and deep. I couldn't help but wonder if his heart and lungs ever got bored due to inactivity. Wee Drop cast an experienced eye around the table, like an invigilator surveying the room just before an exam begins.

'The first round of FoF starts, now!' Stew tapped his palm on the tabletop.

The large, black clock on the wall behind the bar, struck the hour.

7.

'Consider this,' Stew said. 'The American John E. Douglas is an artist famous for painting only profiles of his subjects. One of his paintings, a profile of a Goliath birdeater, sold at Sotheby's for £500,000.'

'I thought there was only one possible fact we had to evaluate,' Thoughtless said. 'There are several in that.'

'Or none at all,' the Fish pointed out.

'The key,' Bean said, 'is to not let our fiendish Card Master confuse you. FoF grew out of the age-old belief that two heads – or more – are better than one. We wanted to see how often that proves to be the case, because usually it is two heads – mine and Jack's – against Stew's.'

'What do your results suggest?'

'It's fifty-fifty. It's worth bearing in mind, though, that Stew knows in advance what he's going to say, and we never do. He can prepare, and we can't. Tonight, of course, it's five heads against one.'

'Wee drop ad or wee drop disad?' Wee Drop said. 'That's the wee drop q.'

'You're right,' I agreed. 'That is the question. Are five heads better than two, or will too many cooks spoil the broth?'

'If we can't work together to beat Stew at this, I don't fancy our chances of catching a serial killer,' Thoughtless said. 'And, what the heck, is a Goliath birdeater?'

'Theraphosa blondi,' I replied. 'The world's largest spider.'

'Largest by mass,' Bean said. 'The giant huntsman spider has the largest leg span.'

'I've seen a spider walk on water,' the Fish said. 'I don't like spiders.'

'You have twenty seconds left,' Stew informed us.

Wee Drop pointed at Bean and myself. 'Wee drop ans,' he ordered.

Bean didn't hesitate. 'Card Master, I have considered what you said, and I would, in a creative response to your paintings reference, like to frame your assertion as fiction.'

'You are correct.' Stew scowled. 'I thought you were going to waste your time talking about eight-legged arthropods.'

'I was just letting everyone have their say,' Bean replied. 'The references to painting and spiders were your deliberate attempts at misdirection. You threw them in hoping they would lead us down the proverbial viam horti.'

'The what?' Thoughtless looked at me.

'Garden path,' I said. 'My good friend likes to show off his Latin from time to time.'

'Anyway,' Bean continued. 'The Card Master was not only trying to misdirect us, he was also being mischievous with his reference to the painting of profiles.'

'Mischievous and relevant,' Stew interjected.

'Indeed,' Bean smiled in acknowledgement. 'John E. Douglas is not a successful artist, but he is an expert on profiles. In fact, he's the man responsible for creating a brand-new approach to his area of study, one that has since been adopted all over the world.'

'Which is?' The Fish slid his hands together as he spoke.

'The profiling of serial killers,' Bean said. 'Douglas was the man who was primarily responsible for creating the FBI's Behavioural Analysis Unit. He was the man who instigated and developed the idea that you could create a profile of a killer from a study of other serial killers and from the actual crime scenes themselves, and that you could then use that profile to catch the killer and so prevent additional deaths.'

'Wee drop psych an,' Wee Drop clarified, for the benefit of anyone around the table who couldn't understand proper words.

'The psych an of p-n-j's,' I confirmed, working on the principle that if you can't beat them, sometimes you might as well join them.

'How does his work offer any lessons for us?' Thoughtless asked. 'None of us are experts on serial killer psychology and we haven't visited the crime scenes.'

'Well, I'd suggest there are two things we can presume about our killer with a high degree of certainty,' Stew said.

'You've been researching this, ever since you came up with the John E. Douglas FoF, haven't you?' Bean said. 'And you knew which card you were picking, even though you wanted us to believe it was a random choice?'

'I guessed that, to get us started, a card game was probably on the cards,' Stew allowed himself a half-smile. 'It seemed, therefore, that the best thing to do was to fix the deck to ensure we started off with something relevant.' Stew glanced at me for approval. I gave him a thumbs-up. He continued quickly. 'And the things we do know about serial killers and about our modern society, lead us, statistically, towards two useful starting points. Firstly, that our killer is male. We can work on that assumption because, of all known serial killers in the last century, only between eleven and twelve percent were women.'

'You're right,' I said. 'Although Bella and Doreen can't tell me who their killer was, they've made it clear it was a man.'

'You could have mentioned that before,' Bean said.

'Sorry, too busy getting the team together.' I shrugged apologetically.

The Paddington Fish sighed. His eyes glazed over.

'Men,' he said. 'Men destroy things. Men are destroying

the seas in so many ways. Overfishing. Pollution. Climate change. When men go out on a boat, they're free to do anything they like. And they do. They abuse rather than respect. One day, the seas will make us all pay for what we are allowing these men to do.'

'Let's just focus on the one man who's killing prostitutes,' Bean said. 'I don't think we can do that and save the planet at the same time.'

The Fish shook his head and came back from whatever watery mess he'd been sinking into.

Bean addressed Stew. 'What's your second starting point?'

'It's simply this,' Stew said. 'We can very reasonably assume that our killer is at least forty-five or fifty years of age, possibly even older.'

'Why is that?' I raced Thoughtless to the question.

'Because of how the different generations have responded to having the Covid vaccine.' Stew looked even more pleased with himself than before. 'You see, we know, anecdotally at least, that the under thirty-fives were far more prone to fainting and panic attacks than the over-fifties. And it wasn't because they feared possible side-effects, it was because they were scared of needles.'

'That's terrible for them,' Thoughtless said. 'Phobias are awful things; they should be offered counselling.'

'They should get a compulsory kick up the bum,' Bean said. 'And being scared of something – like having an injection - doesn't automatically mean you've got a phobia.'

'Jus wee drop f,' Wee Drop agreed.

'What does a fear of needles have to do with our serial killer?' The Fish asked.

'Well, if we think about the terribly violent and bloody nature of the murders,' Stew glanced at me again. 'Sorry,' he mouthed. 'If we consider just how gruesome they were, it's impossible to imagine that they could have been carried out by someone who is terrified of injections. Society has changed drastically in the last few decades. It's much easier to be squeamish now than it ever was. I just can't see a twenty or thirty-something modern adult male having the capacity to do the things our killer has.'

'Are you suggesting that serial killers will become a thing of the past, as the older generation dies out?'

'They're certainly on the decline,' Stew said. 'Research in America shows a significant decrease over the last few decades. It's thought this is due to the growth of forensic science and the fact that people are far more aware, and therefore far less vulnerable, than they used to be.'

'You're saying that our serial killer is even more of a rare breed than he once was?' Thoughtless shifted position slightly.

'Rare? Yes. Serial killer? Technically, he isn't. Not yet. Our guy would be more properly labelled a spree killer. To fit into the category of serial killer, you need to have killed three or more.'

I decided not to mention the other girls who had disappeared. The last thing I wanted to do was create even more pressure.

'However,' Stew continued, 'there is anecdotal evidence that these individuals do kill with ever-increasing frequency. Which means we don't have time to waste.'

It was obvious that the more Stew talked about this, the more fidgety he was becoming. His neck was starting to redden, too. Usually, knowing something that the rest of us didn't, had Stew sticking his chest out like a pigeon performing for a prospective mate.

'What's the problem?' I asked.

Stew was slow to reply. 'It's not like researching other

topics,' he said finally. 'I've only had a couple of hours, just to get ready for this meeting, but it already feels horribly different.'

'Different from what?'

'Learning facts for quizzes. I know I should have understood that this was, well, more real than that, more serious. On one level, of course, I did. I mean, this man's killed two of your friends. Only, when you start to delve into it more deeply, it's just...just...stressful. Not scared-of-having-an-injection stressful, but properly, properly stressful.' Stew looked at each one of us in turn. 'I'm not like the youngsters,' he said. 'Honestly. I'm proper older generation. I just need a little time to adapt.'

'Or just a little help,' Thoughtless said. 'I'm happy to do some yoga with you.'

'I could take you into the pool,' the Fish offered.

'I'll cope, thank you,' Stew replied. 'I'm not going anywhere. I'm in this until we catch him.'

'In that case, let me summarise.' Bean got us back on track. 'We're after a man who's middle-aged or older. That's our starting point.'

'Pity we don ha wee drop cl,' Wee Drop said.

'We don't even know if the police have got any clues,' Bean said. 'And it's not like we can ask them. They'd see us as vigilantes, not helpers.'

'True.' The Fish said. 'We're literally clueless.'

'Clueless,' Thoughtless repeated.

'Clueless,' Stew agreed.

'Only we're not,' I said, remembering suddenly the other thing I should never have forgotten. 'We're not clueless. We're not remotely clueless, I'm just a fool, that's what it is.'

'What are you talking about?' Bean's curiosity was coloured with an obvious tinge of frustration at the possibility that I'd made a time-wasting error.

'We do have a clue, I'd just forgotten it,' I confessed.

'How could you do that?' Bean's curiosity disappeared and only frustration remained. 'First of all, you forgot to tell us that our suspect was a man. Now you're saying that you've got a clue that you haven't thought to share with us!'

'I'm sorry,' I looked to Wee Drop for some understanding. 'I've had a challenging day.'

'Wee drop f,' Wee Drop raised a hand. 'Jus wee drop f.'

'It's not a wee drop of forgetfulness, it's a great dollop of stupidity.' Bean tried to frown, but the wave of frustration was already dissipating in response to Wee Drop's comment.

I wondered what it felt like to be a super-experienced teacher with such power at your disposal. Now, though, wasn't the time to dwell on that.

'I'm sorry,' I said. 'Being honest all day has made me forgetful. It won't happen again.'

'Which bit?' Bean asked. 'Being honest or being forgetful?'

'Both. Neither. The combination. Honestly, I'm doing my best to remember everything I need to.'

'That's all we can ask,' Thoughtless said.

'Let's not waste any more time then,' Bean said. 'What's the clue?'

I told them.

8.

'Dat droll hen.' Bean repeated. 'How do you spell that?' I spelt it out.

Thoughtless asked softly, 'Are you sure it's a real clue?'

'Yeah, absolutely. Doreen didn't mean to say it. She

140

didn't come up with it because she felt pressured into being helpful. She just said it. It was more a subconscious thing than a deliberate effort.'

'We have to treat it as if it's really important,' Bean said. 'It's all we've got, and we can't afford to leave any stone unturned. Dat droll hen might be signposting the way forward, so we need to determine where it's pointing.'

'In that case,' I addressed the SP virgins, 'I'm going to be quizmaster and Stew and Bean are going to be the contestants. You guys are the audience. Only join in if I ask you to.' I didn't give anyone chance to comment. 'Right. Messrs Gardner and Curry, you have sixty seconds to solve our crucial conundrum – although I know you're thinking about it already – and your time starts, now!'

'Bzzz!' Bean pressed the imaginary buzzer almost instantly.

The non-quizzers around the table were open-mouthed with admiration. Stew looked more than a little irritated by the speed of his likely defeat. For reasons that were not obvious, Bean was looking decidedly uncomfortable.

'Mr Curry, what is your answer?'

Bean hesitated.

'I need an immediate answer, or I'll start the clock again.'

'I've got the answer,' Bean spoke so quietly I could barely hear him. 'That's the problem. The answer just jumped out and hit me straight away. I'm certain that it's right.'

'Tell us then, or we'll be forced to conclude that you're buying yourself time.'

'All of you lean in,' Bean said. 'Come in close because I'm not saying this out loud.'

The others looked at Wee Drop and me for direction. We both leant in. They followed suit.

Bean glanced around the room. 'The answer to the dat droll hen conundrum,' he whispered, 'is terrifyingly obvious. When you unscramble dat droll hen you get *the landlord*.'

9.

We finished our drinks in super-fast time, just to make sure everything looked normal, and got out of the pub without saying another word.

'Where shall we go now?' I asked.

'Back to your place,' Bean said. 'Let's get inside 5a, lock the doors, and have a very serious conversation.'

'But the Shades are there!'

'The Shades might be there, but only you can communicate with them. They're not going to make any difference to the rest of us, are they?'

'It's going to complicate things for me.'

'And my answer hasn't?' Even though we were outside, Bean kept his voice down. 'We've just discovered that dat droll hen unscrambled becomes *the landlord*, and Barry, the landlord, is a fifty-five-year-old male, just as Stew predicted! Wouldn't you say that's complicated things enough?'

'You could argue that it's simplified them.'

'What?'

'At least we now have a suspect.'

'A man we've known for years!'

'You've known me for longer, and there was an important thing you didn't know about me.'

'That's a good point,' Stew said. His voice was more than a little shaky, and his right foot looked like it was trying to Boom-Ka-Ka-Chow without letting the rest of his body know. 'But we still need somewhere to go.'

'Ok. Ok.' There were lights on in the upstairs room of the pub. I saw Morgan's shadow through the flimsy curtains. She was joined by an equally recognisable shape. 'Barry's up there,' I said.

'Well, let's go to 5a now,' Stew said quickly. 'Before he looks out of the window and sees us all standing here.'

I had to accept it was the strategically sensible thing to do.

'C'mon then.'

I set off.

Stew made a point of keeping up with me. The others walked a couple of paces behind.

It was a silent journey. I guess everyone was doing whatever they could to get their heads around the possibility that Barry, the landlord, was a spree, and potentially serial, killer.

I ducked the challenge of that, focusing instead on the absolute inappropriateness of the word *spree* to describe a type of killer. Some words should never be used, either to describe people or their behaviours. That's a truth I hold dear. *Spree* is a word that should never be used when talking about murder. A spree is such a jolly sounding thing. In its noun-format, 99.999% of people only use it to describe an unrestrained period of doing something that society encourages. Something like drinking, or shopping, or spending our money on the many other things we don't really need, and which might, in fact, cause us harm.

That sort of spree, the sort that empties out our bank account and leaves us vomiting and headachy surrounded by bags of clothing we'll never wear, people we hadn't met until late last night and stains we can't explain, is a happy, let-me-tell-my-friends-all-about-it kind of spree. It's the sort that most of us do from time to time to make ourselves feel better.

My question is, what kind of forensic-analyst-idiot decided that *spree* should also be used to describe a p-n-j who's currently performing violence at Masters level, but has the potential to progress to a PhD.

'Sorry darling, I won't be home for dinner, I'll be too busy spreeing with extreme violence.' [19]

As we reached 5a, my mind dumped *spree* like it was empty fish and chip papers. My imagination stepped up without missing a beat and forced me to picture what was about to happen.

On the one hand: Bella, Doreen, and Darius. Three Shades who could only be seen and heard by me. All of whom were expecting me to be leading an elite team in the immediate pursuit and capture of a violent killer.

On the other hand: Bean Curry, Stew Gardner, Wee Drop, Thoughtless and the Paddington Fish. Two drunken quizzing superstars, a former schoolteacher who was more than a few syllables short of a sentence, a yoga and meditation devotee, more at home in an ashram than a pub, and a former diver more at home under the water than out of it, who breathed in and out only once every full moon.

In-between the two hands: me, like an inflated paper bag, just waiting to be popped.

A part of me wished we'd just stormed into the upstairs room at the pub and accused Barry of killing two prostitutes. In fact, we could have told him outright that we knew it was him and that we were making a citizen's arrest.

---

[19] *Spreeing* is the rarely used verb version. If it seems unusual to you, just remind yourself of everything that's gone before, and you'll realise it falls well short of the weird-field.

It would have been six against one.

And, whilst I was pretty sure that Thoughtless was a pacifist, and I knew for a fact that neither Bean, Stu nor myself had ever hit anyone in our lives, there was something about the Paddington Fish that was undeniably frightening, and I was sure that Wee Drop never backed down. So, we'd have been Ok. And one way or another, we'd have reached some form of conclusion. If only for a while.

As it was, we'd got nowhere.

Well, that wasn't quite true.

We'd got to 5a.

I opened the door and led the way in.

10.

The Shades were shocked wordless by the gang of disparates that traipsed into the lounge and commandeered the chairs. (Apart from Thoughtless, who sat on the floor.)

Their state of wordless shock lasted for all of five seconds. Not surprisingly, Bella spoke first.

'What's going on?'

'I brought the team back home with me.'

'I can see that.'

'We need somewhere private where we can plan our next move.'

'You and the team?' Bella waved a dismissive, disbelieving hand in the direction of the five faces that were staring at me talking into thin air.

'Yeah, me and the team.'

'These are the people who are going to help you catch...him?'

'Yeah.'

'This is the best you could do?'

'It's a well-balanced team.'

'Oh, I can see that. I saw that as soon as they walked in. I took one look and thought to myself, Jack's only gone and created a modern-day Justice League of America.' Bella's sarcasm dripped like water from a leaky tap.

For the sake of my team who, unlike the Shades, could only hear one half of the conversation, I kept my voice calm. 'Everyone's got their own unique talent. You'd be surprised.'

Bella jabbed a finger at Thoughtless. 'When was the ability to sit with one leg on top of the other upgraded to a superpower?'

'At about the same time that gratitude was found to be in short supply.'

That earned me a finger jab. 'You feel gratitude when someone's done something good for you! Like when you help a chicken cross the road. It doesn't feel grateful until you've got it across safely.'

'It isn't a chicken you help to cross the road, it's an old person.'

'Which road were you at?' Bella snorted like an angry horse. 'You don't help old people cross the road unless they ask, everyone knows that. If you just suddenly grab a pensioner by the arm and march them across the road you could terrify them. They could die on you.'

'Don't you think that, when you grab a chicken by the wing and start walking, you make it even more terrified than it already was?'

'What do you mean, even more terrified?'

'Chickens are always terrified. That's the price they pay for being a chicken. That's why they walk like they do. Like they're walking on hot coals whilst being constantly surprised by foxes going Boo!'

I thought that would throw Bella into a state of confusion and bring this particularly absurd conversation to an end. I couldn't have been more wrong.

'That proves it then,' she said triumphantly.

'Proves what?'

'Chickens only want to cross the road because they're trying to escape. It's right that we should help them, and it's no wonder they'd be grateful.'

'Bella, please! It isn't chickens, it's old people!'

'Old people don't try to escape. When they go, they go, but until then they're happy enough sitting in a chair with a blanket over their legs watching daytime tele.'

'Why are you talking about chickens?' Bean asked. 'We're not scared. We wouldn't have agreed to help if we were scared.'

'I'm scared,' Stew said.

'Not scared enough to have said "No",' Bean said.

'I was more scared of saying "No",' Stew said.

'Fear can't exist in a mind that's living in the moment,' Thoughtless stretched effortlessly.

'And if you do start to feel it, you can always breathe it out,' the Fish said.

'Wee drop bl,' Wee Drop added.

'What did he just say?' Bella asked.

I translated. 'He said you can blow out your fear.'

'How do you do that?' It was Doreen's turn to join in.

'You need a great teacher.'

At which point, Bella and Doreen simultaneously shut up, stared at Wee Drop, and then stepped back a pace.

They looked at each other, looked back at Wee Drop, and then nodded, their mouths opening.

'It is, isn't it?' Doreen said.

'It definitely is,' Bella confirmed. 'All day long.'

'Oh my God!' Doreen clasped her face in disbelief. 'It's

him! I didn't recognise him at first!'

'Who is who? I asked.[20]

'Him,' Doreen pointed. 'He was our History teacher. Best there ever was.'

'Can't argue with that,' Bella said. 'He didn't let you get away with anything, but he helped you out when you needed it. Especially when you most needed it.' Bella reddened.

I couldn't help but wonder what Wee Drop had done to help the teenage Bella. Now, though, was not the time to ask, or to confuse the situation further by reintroducing the two dead ex-pupils to their teacher.

'If Sir has promised to help you, you've definitely got more chance than I first gave you credit for.' Bella nodded as she spoke.

Doreen joined in. 'I swear he can see round corners.'

'He can see inside your mind.' Bella's eyes moistened. Then she stamped her right foot, shook her body, and turned all her attention back to me. 'Ok. What are the others good at?'

'Problem-solving, staying calm under pressure, adapting. All the things we need.'

'And they didn't agree to help because they were drunk?'

'Some of them don't even touch alcohol.'

'How weird is that?'

'Can I just say,' Darius stepped forward. He had barely

---

[20] I know, I should have said, 'whom?' but it's hard to be linguistically accurate when you're having your first go at managing a meeting between three Shades and a motley Justice League of America crew, who have come together in pursuit of a spree killer.

taken his eyes off me since we'd all entered 5a. 'Can I just say that, although I'm not a victim of anything other than my own imagination, and none of these people were ever my teacher, I am truly grateful.'

'What are you grateful for?' Doreen asked.

'For the fact that people who don't know us – who'll never know us – are willing to help. Let's remember, they can't even see us, and they're still here. Not everyone's bad.'

Doreen shared a meaningful look with her blond friend. 'That's the truth,' she said. 'Imagine if they did those adverts on tele for starving kids in Africa, but they didn't show you the kids? No one would give anything.'

'Yeah. Most people have got to see the flies in their eyes.' Bella cast her own light-blues over my team. 'Tell them that we really appreciate their help. Not just for us, but for the girls they're going to save. Tell them that we're sorry we can't help any more than we have.'

'Would you care to give us an update?' Bean asked, before I could pass on Bella's message.

'Bella, Doreen and Darius really do appreciate the commitment you're all making,' I said. 'It's just taken them a few moments to adjust to your presence.'

'I'd have thought Shades were used to adjusting,' Bean said. 'After all, they've already made one massive adjustment.'

'They've transitioned. It doesn't mean they've necessarily adjusted,' I said. 'And, like I suggested before, I think there are other places to go, beyond where they are now. They still face the uncertainty of that.'

'But you don't know that for sure?'

'No. Bella wasn't the first Shade I ever met, but she was the first to move into 5a. She's the only Shade I've spent so much time with, and even she doesn't know what happens next.'

'Maybe this it?' Stew said. 'Maybe 5a is Heaven?'

'Or Hell?' Bean sat down. 'I have to say, it would be reassuring to know that 5a is as bad as it gets. That living with you is the worst thing eternity has to offer.'

'It needn't be either,' The Fish offered the third alternative. 'This could be Purgatory.'

My fellow quizzers kicked into gear in an instant.

'Purgatorio,' Stew said, 'is the second part of **Dante**'s **Divine Comedy**, written in the early fourteenth century.'

'It's described as a mountain in the Southern Hemisphere,' Bean took over. 'It's got Ante-Purgatory at its base, then seven terraces, each connected with one of the deadly sins, and -'

'– The Earthly Paradise at the top,' Stew finished it for him.

The pair of them stopped talking and looked around the room like two jaded estate agents.

'I don't think there's space for the seven terraces,' Stew said.

'I doubt he's got a third bedroom upstairs, let alone an Earthly Paradise.' Bean turned to the Fish. 'I think we can safely say that Purgatory is out of the question.'

Bella looked at me in disbelief. 'When are they going to start doing whatever it is you came here to do?'

'Sir never have let his class waste time,' Doreen said.

'But this isn't his class,' Bella replied. 'This is Jack's, so Sir is being polite and waiting for him to sort it.'

'Well, I'm not Sir and this isn't a classroom,' I said. I wanted to point out also that, with her comments about chickens, Bella was as guilty of wasting time as anyone else. Instead, I said, 'What's happening is that they're getting themselves into the best possible mind-set. They're like

150

athletes, warming up before the big race.'

Neither of the girls looked convinced.

'What are the Shades saying?' It was Thoughtless who asked.

'They, er, wondered when we're going to start planning.'

'Right now.' Bean shifted into his quizzing pose. 'I think our starting point is fairly obvious. Jack, you need to tell the Shades what we've discovered and ask them if they've got any additional insights, or information, they can share with us.'

'That's a good starting point,' the Fish agreed.

'What have you discovered?' Bella asked before I could say anything. 'Why is it a good starting point?'

I coughed, mainly because of my inevitable nervous tension, and partly to give the impression that I was, finally, bringing the meeting to order.

Everyone fell silent. When I spoke, I looked only at Bella.

'We've had what we believe to be a breakthrough,' I said. 'Stew has gathered some useful data about the profile of the killer and, more than that, we've also solved the dat droll hen conundrum.'

Darius sat down. Doreen gasped. Bella ignored them both and stared at me. Her eyes switched into full-spotlight mode. I couldn't help but blink and turn my face away.

'We need to share this with you,' I said, 'because, well, a) you deserve to know where we're at and b) we're hoping that it might free you to help us again. Are you ready?'

Darius and Doreen nodded in unison. Bella watched me intensely. The heat on my face increased. I forced myself to turn back into the glare, and let my mouth do the talking.

11.

Bella interrupted me when I was only halfway through.

'You mean Barry, the landlord of The Frog & Bull? You've come home to carry on your meeting, because you think Barry is the man who killed us?'

'Yes and yes.' I watched my Shade-sister closely. 'Now that I've said his name, can you tell me if it was him?'

Bella and Doreen exchanged glances. They shook their heads simultaneously.

'Does that mean you don't know,' I asked, 'or that you can't say?'

'Both. Neither.' Bella squinted. 'This isn't a quiz. We can't just give you the winning answer. Things work differently for us. You know that.'

'It was a fair question,' I said.

Bella shook her head. 'You and the Justice League need go about this in your own way. If Doreen and me knew how to tell you who killed us, we would. But we don't. So you just have to get on with it.'

'Well, that's why we're here,' I said. 'Dat droll hen is *the landlord*, and the only landlord we know who fits the profile is Barry.'

'There must be loads of other landlords who are forty-five or older,' Bella pointed out.

'We've got to start somewhere,' I explained. 'We have to go through some sort of process of elimination.'

'The killer's going through a process of elimination. You need to be going through a process of trapping and catching.'

'In order to identify who the killer is, we've first got to determine who he isn't.'

Bella looked up at the ceiling in exasperation. 'You don't have to know all the people someone isn't before you can discover who they really are. When I first met Darius, and you told me he was Darius, I didn't have to go and visit all the other single men in town, just to make sure that he wasn't one of them and that he really was Darius.'

'Sometimes,' I said, as patiently as I could manage, 'to find out what the truth really is, you must identify and study all the things that might be true and discount them one-by-one until there's only one left. That one is the truth. So, if you're searching for one person – the one needle in the haystack – you have to identify and discount all the people it might be until you're left with only one. By definition, that's the person you're after.'

'But if there's only one needle in the haystack, all you do is look for the needle and ignore the hay. You don't waste time checking that the hay isn't a needle. Hay's hay, and a needle's a needle. Just tell the search party that they're looking for a needle, don't even mention the hay.' Bella turned to Doreen. 'Why do men have to complicate everything?'

'It helps them think they're in charge.' Doreen answered without hesitation. 'My Mum taught me that.'

'Your Mum was right, girl.'

'Tell me about it.'

'Look,' I tried again, 'I accept that, as men, we might occasionally over-complicate things and, on behalf of men, I apologise.' I had one final go at explaining our strategy to my sometime-fiery Shade-sister. 'As a quizzer, there are times when you're asked a question and, because you're not sure of the answer, your mind comes up with several possible answers. What you do then, is go through the answers working out which ones are wrong and why. When you've done that, the one you're left with, is the right answer. It's the same with identifying the killer.'

'Why is the last answer always the right one?'

'Because you've determined that all the others are wrong.'

Bella shook her head angrily. 'What I don't get, is why you always leave the right answer 'till the end. If you know the last answer is always going to be the right one, why don't you just choose the last answer first?'

'It's not just about what the right answer is, it's equally about what it isn't.' Darius stood up as he spoke. He'd been silent and still for so long, I think we'd all forgotten he was there. 'Sometimes what isn't, is the most important thing there is.'

'What are you talking about?' Bella's exasperation shifted up a few degrees. 'How can something that isn't something be the most important something? If something isn't there, it doesn't exist! If something isn't something, it isn't anything! Everyone can see that.'

For once, Darius wasn't fazed by Bella's sudden shift of mood.

'I'm not asking you to believe me. But Eliot knew about these things, and he used it in his poems. It's about understanding the ultimate meaning of life by understanding the power of nothingness, knowing what isn't, rather than what is. It's spiritual.'

'Can you please keep us involved in what's going on?' Once again, Bean was the spokesman for the human contingent.

'Yeah. Sure. Sorry.' I had no idea where to start, so I chose the end. 'Darius was just talking about T. S. Eliot and what he had to say about the importance of knowing what isn't.'

'Wow!' Stew applauded. 'Darius knows about the negativities, the nothingness, of Eliot's early poems and how he used the Christian via negativia? That's incredible!'

'Well, he didn't quite put it like that, but, yeah, he's a big Eliot fan.'

'Eliot doesn't have fans, he has readers, and students, and thinkers,' Darius said, with just a hint of indignation in his voice.

'Sounds like he has overthinkers,' Bella said.

'Thinking is good for the mind,' Darius countered.

'Imagination's better,' Bella said.

Stew grabbed Bean's forearm. 'Maybe when this is all over, we could get Darius to join us on quiz night? He's got to know more than just Eliot. People who read Eliot nearly always like Blake and Milton and Whitman. Sometimes Shakespeare, too. Imagine if we'd got Darius with us, whispering answers to Jack?'

'He wouldn't have to whisper,' I pointed out.

'We'd be breaking the rules,' Bean said sternly.

'Wee drop ch,' Wee Drop confirmed in his exam-invigilator voice.

'And we don't cheat,' Bean went on. 'We win fairly and squarely or not at all.'

'If people focused less on winning and more on just *being*, the world would be a happier place,' Thoughtless said, moving effortlessly into some sort of forward bend.

'*Doing* is what matter most,' the Fish said, looking deliberately at his oversized diver's wristwatch. 'Doing the right thing at the right time.'

'At least one of you is making sense,' Bella said, addressing my makeshift J L of A. 'While you're all sat here talking, the killer might be out there looking for another girl! He might have already...found one. Right? He might be doing that...that stuff he does, right now! And if he isn't, he soon will be. Whatever it is that you know, or you don't know, or you don't need to know, we do all know that he'll be doing that. So can you please get up, go out and catch him?' She turned her attention back to me. 'Tell them.'

'The Fish is right, time isn't on our side,' I said. 'Bella and the Shades are desperate for us to start looking for him before another girl dies.'

Bean nodded. 'Let's have a very focused ten minutes and then we roll.'

'I think the only of us who can roll is Thoughtless,' I couldn't stop myself.

'I can roll,' the Fish said.

'A focused ten minutes!' Bean cut off the impending meander. 'Ten minutes of intense planning, brains as focused as if we were quizzing under pressure, and then we go! Fish, time us.'

'Will do.' The Fish checked his watch. 'Time starts now,' he said, pressing a button.

12.

Bean didn't waste a second. 'Jack, ask the girls if they know what their killer looked like.'

'I've been through this with them before,' I said.

'He's been through this with us before!' Bella shouted.

'Do it again,' Bean insisted. 'It might make a difference now that they know we have a prolife that fits Barry.'

I asked the girls.

Doreen shook her head. Bella checked out the ceiling again.

'He was wearing a black Covid mask,' Doreen said. 'He never took it off.'

'You didn't tell me that before.'

'Didn't think it mattered. I'd have just been telling you that I didn't see his face. What use is that?'

'Jack probably thinks it's important,' Bella said. 'He probably thinks that he needs to know everything we didn't

156

see, so that, when he's eliminated all of that, he'll be left with what we did see,'

Bella's dog-with-a-bone attitude was one of those things that made me love and fear and admire and need her all at the same time.

'Didn't you think it was unusual that he had a mask on?'

'No,' Doreen looked surprised by my question. 'It makes no difference to us what they're wearing, and the girls who are real professionals don't do tongues anyway.'

'Making any progress?' Bean asked.

'No. They didn't see his face.'

'What about the rest of him? Size, shape, any distinguishing features?'

I asked and got knocked back as I knew I would.

'No matter what we tried earlier, we couldn't get passed that door,' Bella said. 'You do remember how hard we tried, don't you?'

'Of course. I remember everything you've ever told me and everything you've ever done whilst you've been here.'

'No, you don't. You've got a memory like a sieve for everything apart from answers for quiz questions.'

'Not true. I do remember.'

Bella raised an eyebrow. The Fish coughed and tapped his watch. The clock was ticking.

'It's not that I don't remember,' I said quickly. 'It's just that I also forget. Now, let's get back to the killer. Is there anything you can do to tell us something more about him?'

Bella sighed deeply. 'We'll give it one more go,' she said.

The two Shades closed their eyes. They didn't move or speak for at least a minute.

Finally, Doreen said, 'I just can't. It's like there's nothing to get hold of, but he's in there somewhere, in the nothingness.'

'That's exactly right,' Bella said. 'He's in the

nothingness.'

Temptation shone brightly through an open door. It took everything I had to stop myself from reminding Bella what Darius had said about the power of nothingness.

Somehow, I managed to ask, 'How about his voice? Sometimes we can hear something, even if we can't see it. Sometimes we can access or remember sounds, better than we can images. Sounds can be heard even through a door. Can either of you tell us anything about his voice?'

They both closed their eyes and tried again.

'Nope. I can't hear nothing,' Doreen said. She brightened suddenly. 'I did get dat droll hen right, though.'

'You certainly did.' I offered a quick smile. 'Bella, could you hear anything?'

'No. It's silent this side of the door as well as the other side. You'd need ears as good as yours to have a chance of catching anything.'

'Has he got good ears?' Doreen looked genuinely interested.

Bella nodded.

'Do think that's why he hears us?'

'Could be.'

'Three minutes to go,' the Fish said.

'Keep going,' Bean urged. 'Ask them the next thing.'

'What is the next thing?' I asked.

'How should I know?' Bean looked at the others for help.

'The problem is,' Stew said, 'we're question-answerers, that's what we're best at. We're not good at asking the questions.'

He's right,' Bean admitted. 'We're not good at that.'

We all fell silent. The Shades stilled. Nothing changed until the Fish said, 'Two minutes to go.'

Then Wee Drop stood up. He looked round the room.

Bella and Doreen straightened automatically. For one crazy moment, I thought he could see them.

Wee Drop inhaled deeply, considered, nodded, and said, 'We need wee drop hel fr per who wri the ques.'

For the three quizzers present, the realisation hit like a Mike Tyson left hook.

'He's so right,' Bean whispered. 'It's not a question of who we are and what we can do, but who we are not and who we need.'

'Precisely,' I couldn't help but look at Bella. 'When you clear out all the hay, all you're left with is the shiny bright needle. You're left with the person who writes the questions.'

'And that's our very own Morgan le Fay,' Stew completed our teamwork. 'We need to ask her to help us. We need a wee drop of help from the person who writes the quiz.'

At which point everyone looked at me.

13.

My phone call was received with an obvious mix of surprise and pleasure. This turned into a quiet sense of curiosity and confusion when I said that we needed to meet urgently – and not in The Frog & Bull.

Morgan suggested her place. I did my best to thank her without sounding desperate. Fifteen minutes later I was knocking on the door of her traditional mid-terraced house. She let me in, gestured for me to sit down in a cottage style, floral patterned armchair, and somewhat self-consciously tugged her jumper down over her hips as she stood in front of me.

'So,' she said. 'This isn't what I was expecting after our conversation earlier.'

'Me neither.'

'Then...?'

'Well, I, er...' I leant forward in my chair, rubbing both palms over my thighs. 'There are things about me that I wanted to share with you, you know, one night over a few drinks.'

'And now they can't wait?'

'No.'

'Which question should I ask first?'

'I'm sorry?'

'Should I ask, "What are the things about yourself that you need to share with me?" Or should I start with, "Why can't this wait?"'

'Oh. I see.' The question writer and quiz master was doing what came naturally. I was reminded that I had to do the same. Being a psychic medium and a writer, means that I see and hear what other people can't. In many ways, I'd always treated that like a curse, a stigma to hide away, rather than the strength it could be. Earlier tonight Morgan had told me that she believed in the power of the invisible. Now I had to tell her – convince her – that she was right. After all, I was the expert at seeing and communicating with invisible beings.

'Well?' Morgan was waiting patiently for me to choose. 'Which question comes first?'

I pointed to the two-seater settee facing my chair. 'Please, sit down. You don't need to ask either question, I'll answer them both regardless. And, as this isn't a quiz – and, you need to know that, if it was, you couldn't write a question about this topic that would challenge me – but, as it isn't a quiz, I'm going to begin with a reminder, not an answer. Is that Ok?'

'Y – Yes.' Morgan sat.

'Good. Thank you. Now, you told me that you split up

with Thaddeus because you trusted your instinct, because something you couldn't see and couldn't quite explain told you it was the right thing to do. You spoke of how you trusted the invisible.'

'Yes, but I don't see what that has to do with -'

I raised my hand. Morgan stopped talking.

'I'm an expert in the invisible,' I said. 'I might be the world's leading expert.'

Morgan's eyes widened. Her mouth stayed closed.

'I have a friend, Darius – well, he's maybe more of a lodger than a friend – and he would love what you're saying about the importance and power of the invisible. He's obsessed with Eliot, you see, and -'

'- Since when did you have a lodger?' Morgan looked as if she was going to jump back to her feet. Thankfully, she didn't.

'That's the point,' I said. 'He's not the only one. There are two others living in 5a with me. I think of one of them as my sister.'

'What?' This time Morgan did jump to her feet.

'The thing is, they are all what you might call ghosts. They are what I call Shades. They are the spirits of the dead.'

Morgan sat down as quickly as she had stood up.

I kept talking.

Morgan listened without interrupting.

When I finished, her questions were precise and well-sequenced.

When I had answered them all to her satisfaction, she sat back in the settee and reflected silently for a couple of minutes. Then she said,

'You really are an expert.'

'Yes.' It sounded strange, but felt good, to hear my mouth say that.

'I believe you completely,' Morgan said. 'I totally accept that you are a psychic medium, and that you and the others have committed to catching a killer. What I still don't understand is why you were so insistent that we met away from The Frog & Bull?'

'It's because of Barry,' I said, trying my best to keep my breathing and voice on an even keel.

'Uncle Barry?'

'Yes.'

'What does he have to do with any of this?'

'We have a clue. It's our only clue, but it's a really strong one.'

'And?'

'And it points us very firmly in his direction.'

'What do you mean?' Morgan's fists clenched as she spoke.

'He's our suspect.'

'That's impossible!' The clenched fists came up to either side of her mouth.

'We only have one suspect, and it's him. I'm sorry.'

'That doesn't mean he's the killer – and he couldn't be anyway! I know he doesn't seem to, but he really cares! He really does!' Morgan fought to hold her tears back.

'The best way to prove his innocence is for us to investigate thoroughly, without saying anything to the police. I don't want it to be him either.'

That was the truth. I wasn't just terrified of destroying my relationship with Morgan before it had begun, I didn't want the killer to be someone I knew. I didn't want to confront the fact that my clever eyes could see Shades, and find humour where others couldn't, but had failed to recognise a killer when they saw one.

Morgan's hands had opened. They were cupping her face as she leaned forwards, her elbows on her knees. I

162

could see her mind working frantically to identify the next, most useful question. I gave her the time she needed.

Finally, she said, 'So, what exactly do you need from me?'

'I – we – need to know what to ask the Shades, to see if we can get more information from them.'

Morgan nodded. She considered only briefly. 'I'm not coming back to 5a with you,' she said. 'I'm not going to actively join your...your team.'

'I understand.'

She stood up, looking out of the lounge windows rather than at me. Her jumper was riding up over her hips. She didn't notice.

She told me what I needed to know.

14.

'The lesson I learnt from Morgan,' I said to the motley crew and the Shades gathered in my front room, 'Is that all we've done so far is ask the Shades about the killer.'

'And why is that a lesson, rather than a simple statement of fact?' Bean asked.

'The learning is that we should frame our questions differently.'

'How?'

'Instead of asking about the killer, we should ask the girls if they know anything about Barry. If they're not being asked about their deaths, they might be able to tell us something.'

'That makes sense,' Bean said.

'Morgan le Fay sharing her magic,' Stew added.

Bella spoke before I could reply. I had the sense that she had been released in some way.

'Barry is well-known by the working girls, especially

163

those who work the park and the streets on the far side,' she said, almost spilling over the words. 'Not by Doreen and me because we had a different patch. I have no idea what he's into – we tend to keep our own secrets - but I know for sure that he goes out late most nights of the week, unless he has a lock-in.'

'Yeah, that's right,' Doreen said, stepping up to stand shoulder-to-shoulder with her friend. 'It could be that he liked it rough, and it got out of control. Who knows?'

I swallowed as adrenaline flooded into my system. 'Doreen, are you saying that because you know for a fact that Barry liked it rough, and that it got out of control?'

Doreen blinked. She looked to Bella for help. My Shade-sister shrugged her shoulders and gestured vaguely. Doreen retreated a pace. 'I...I can't answer that,' she said.

'Because my question was about your killer?'

'It's 'cos I don't know.' Doreen took another step back. If she'd had a physical body, she would have bumped into Darius. As it was, he still stepped abruptly to one side. 'I don't know what it is that I don't know, because what I do know – the most important stuff – is on the other side of that door.'

'Of course. I understand. I'm sorry for letting myself ask the wrong question again.' I offered what I hoped was a reassuring smile. 'But you do both know for sure that Barry spends a lot of time, late at night, with working girls?'

'Absolutely!' Bella and Doreen answered one after the other.

When I told the crew what I had learnt, something different happened. Something changed. The way they all looked at each other, and then back at me, and then into the space where the Shades were standing. The way they all retreated somewhere inside themselves. The way no one wanted to speak.

164

'What's happened to them?' Bella asked.

'Reality,' I said. 'It's just giving them all a big squeeze.'

'What about you?'

'It squeezed me earlier, before I went out and asked them to help.'

'What does it mean?' Doreen asked.

'It means it's all become real now.'

'It was real before.' Doreen frowned. 'If it wasn't real, Bella and me wouldn't be here.'

'You're right. Of course you are. It's just a bit more complicated than that.' I tried to explain. 'You know how there's different stages of life – babies, teenagers, grownups, Shades – well, in the same way, there's different stages of knowing something's real. You can think you know something's real, and you can make decisions based on that, and then you reach a point, or something happens, and you realise that it's far more real than you realised it was. That's when you realise what you're really doing.'

'For a man who write short jokes, you do use a lot of words sometimes,' Bella gave Doreen a knowing look. 'He's just a man making things complicated again. Remember when we first went on the game?'

'Yep.'

'Thought we knew what we were getting into?'

'Yep.'

'Didn't have a clue, though, did we?'

'Nope.'

'And then, before you knew it, you were making a stranger happy, and wishing you'd got a bar job instead?'

'Yep.'

'That's the position they're in now.'

'Got ya.' Doreen did a quick survey of my still self-absorbed crew. 'I reckon they'd have struggled working the street.'

165

Sometimes I just wanted to tell them both how sorry I was that they'd grown up in such a terrible world, run by people who didn't know and didn't care about the reality of life on the streets, surrounded by people who didn't give them a second glance.

When lockdown rules ended, I heard lots of folk saying how they'd missed being with people in the flesh. I was the opposite. I'd preferred spending time with those without flesh. For all the complications and complexities of managing relationships with Shades, it still seems to me that it's those who have flesh who cause far more harm in the world than those who don't. [21]

'We stopped watching the clock ages ago,' the Fish said suddenly. 'We're running very late.'

And everyone started talking at once.

15.

Wee Drop settled us all down by raising his teacher's magic hand.

Then Bean took over.

'If Barry was having a lock-in tonight, we'd have heard about it. So, in all probability, he'll be going out to visit one of the girls.'

'Then we have to go looking for him,' Thoughtless said.

'That's the inescapable conclusion,' Stew said.

'It's time to take the plunge,' the Fish agreed.

A part of me wanted to ask the Fish if he chose diving-related language deliberately, but a more powerful part told me to keep quiet. It was a part I was becoming

---

[21] When I say I'd preferred spending time with those without flesh, I mean, of course, Bella.

increasingly used to.

I took a deep breath and said, 'We need to split up, so that we can cover more area. There's one of him and six of us, we need to make that count.'

'Couldn't agree more,' Bean said. 'We have two things in our favour. The first is that he doesn't know we're after him. The second is that we outnumber him. That means we have the element of surprise and extra resources in our favour. If this was a war, we'd be odds-on to win it.'

'That would be true if we were professionals,' Stew said. 'Only we're not. We don't have a professional at this sort of thing amongst us. At best, we have some related skills. The problem is none of us have ever applied them in this context. We're about to go hunting a violent man who gets off on killing other human beings. Let's take a moment to think about that. The consequences of us getting this wrong are huge, potentially catastrophic.'

'I'm scared, too,' I said.

I'd wanted to say that we were all scared, but I didn't think we all were. It seemed that Wee Drop had turned this entire experience into an extreme playground scrap, that Thoughtless had lost any sense of fear somewhere between Downward Dog and a Headstand, and that the Fish was just, well, cold but in a caring way. As for Bean and Stew, they were responding as I'd expected them to.

'I didn't say that just because I'm scared,' Stew replied. 'I'm scared because I don't want to be hurt or killed, and I don't want any of you to be hurt or killed, and I don't want any more women to be killed. That's why I'm scared. I said what I did, though, because it's true. It's a truth we need to address.

'Jack, Bean, and I have seen so many teams of quizzers come onto the scene filled with confidence, sure they could beat us, arrogant even, and we've destroyed them without

167

even breaking sweat. They didn't know how out of their depth they were until it was too late. We can't afford to make that mistake.'

'We won't,' Bean said confidently. 'Will we Jack?'

I hadn't expected that. The best I could manage was, 'Definitely not. No. We're not going to make that sort of mistake. Not at all.'

'Bad place to be – out of your depth,' the Fish said.

'That's why we won't go there,' I said. 'What we have to do now is focus on our strengths, not our weaknesses.'

'And just because Barry – if, indeed, it is Barry – is violent with women, it doesn't mean that he will attempt to be violent with us,' Bean added.

'That's actually a fair point.' Stew lightened a little. 'The most successful serial killers were like marketing professionals. You know, they did their research and targeted specific individuals. They didn't just kill at random.'

'All the more reason why we can split up, as Jack suggested, and go looking for him,' Bean said. 'I think the obvious thing is for us three quizzers to work together,' Bean gestured briefly towards Stew and me, 'and for you three to do the same.'

Wee Drop spoke on behalf of the other two. 'Wee drop pl,' he said.

I was quick to reinforce the point. 'I think it's a great plan,' I said. 'Now all we have to do, is decide where each team should go, how we should keep in touch, and what we should do if one team actually finds Barry.'

Incredibly, that only took us a couple of minutes.

'I can't imagine how we'd manage this if we didn't all have mobile phones,' I said.

'That's why Jack the Ripper got away with it,' Stew said. 'They didn't have the technology to catch him.'

168

'Let's not talk about J the R, eh?' I gave Stew a look that said, "That wasn't a very sensitive comment in front of two prostitutes who were themselves stabbed to death by a modern-day p-n-j."

Stew responded by asking if I needed to go to the loo.

'No. Why?'

'You looked like you were in pain.'

'I'm not in pain.'

'Ok.' Stew turned to the others. 'Does anyone else need to go to the loo before we set off?'

'Hey! It's my loo you're offering out here!'

'Be bad to get caught short.'

'We'll all be fine.' Bean spoke on behalf of everyone's bits and bowels.

'Exactly. Now, let's get going.'

'I need a word with you before you leave,' Bella said, as I started moving everyone to the front door.

I recognised the tone in her voice and knew better than to argue. 'If you'll all just wait outside for a minute,' I said to the team. 'I, er, need to say one last thing to the Shades.'

'What thing?' Bean asked.

'Just a thing, a personal thing,' I said to Bean. 'I'll be quick.'

'Good.' Bean led the team outside.

I shut the door behind them.

'What is it?' I asked.

Bella took a step towards me. 'Do you think it's true, what Bean and Stew said about you all being safe from the killer because he's only after girls like us?'

'I think it makes a lot of sense. Why?'

'I don't see why, if you surround him, he'd just give himself up. I wouldn't if I was a killer.'

'If you wanted to be sure I was safe, you should have told me to leave this to the police.'

'I wasn't thinking about you.'

'You're thinking about the others?'

'I'm thinking that no more working girls deserve to die.'

'You don't deserve anything bad to happen to you either,' Doreen said to me. 'You've got to make sure you come back.'

'We need you here with us,' Darius added. 'When this is all over, we need the four us back together.'

'This is our home now,' Doreen said softly as Bella backed away.

'I, er, I'm not sure what to say.'

I said that because I really wasn't sure. I understand Bella, I know how she operates, but I hadn't expected this from the other two. This was the nearest thing to family care that I'd experienced since my parents died, and I'm only starting to learn how to be good at responding to care. Somehow it was the best timing and the worst timing, all at the same time.

'I, er, will definitely make sure that I come home safe.'

Doreen reached her right palm out towards my chest. 'Promise?'

'Definitely.'

I left without saying another word.

The J L of A were watching me closely as I closed and locked the front door.

'Are you crying?' Bean asked.

'Nope.'

'Looks like it.'

'Wee drop t,' Wee Drop said.

'There are no tears,' I said, wiping my eyes.

'Emotions are the most natural of all expressions,' Thoughtless said. 'We're meant to share them. All of them, even fear.'

'It isn't that,' I said.

Stew jumped in before I could say anymore.

'"Courage isn't the absence of fear, but the triumph over it,"' he said. '"The brave man is not he who does not feel afraid, but he who conquers that fear."'

'Nelson Mandela,' Bean said. 'He adapted it from an earlier quote by Franklin J. Roosevelt. Proof that there's nothing new under the sun.'

'There's nothing new, there's just doing something for the first time,' the Fish said. He pointed into the night. 'Shall we?'

We all looked at each other and nodded.

'Wee drop g,' Wee Drop ordered.

And go we all did.

Dat droll hen

1.

'Hope is the mongrel of emotions,
part need and desperation
part belief and desire
yet, like all mongrels, hope contains the best of
difference:
hope is hardy,
growing strong and living long
on the merest of scraps,
a common companion,
a necessary protector when all seems lost;
when hope is at our heel
we are only one step away from faith.'

Epiah Khan

Wee Drop, Thoughtless and the Paddington Fish, or Team Beta, as we called them, set off towards Forest Road. Bean, Stew and myself[22] headed for the so-called parkland east of the city centre.

It had once been an area of natural beauty, where families congregated, letting their children play and their friendly, soft-mouthed dogs run free. Now, with the nearby large, Victorian houses turned into flats and bedsits, the lack of lighting, and the Council's apparent encouragement of fly-tipping as a social pastime, it was more appropriate for dogging than dog walking. And it was a popular place for the local girls to work.

Bella never had. She preferred the security of

---

[22] Team Alpha, obviously.

streetlights and passing traffic. She said she'd sooner meet someone on the street and take them home. Yet still she had fallen victim to the killer.

I started talking just to stop the thoughts from depressing me.

'When we get there, do we spread out or stay together?' I didn't direct the question at either of them in particular, but Stew automatically waited for Bean to answer.

'We stay together,' he said. 'Our strength is in our teamwork. We make our way through all the most obvious spots, as if we're just a group of normal guys taking a short cut across the park.'

'Normal guys don't ever use the park,' Stew said. 'Especially at this time of night.'

'Drunk normal guys would,' I said. 'They'd use it to save some time, take a pee, spy on some sex-play over an Astra.'

Conversation dried after that. We didn't speak again until we reached the park. It was a dark, desolate place, with a stench that threatened to soak into your clothes and a morbid sense of otherworldliness that hung in the air like a camouflage net.

2.

Tonight, that camouflage net was acting like an echo chamber. As we crossed the concreted area that served as both a car park and a dumping ground for those who had something to dump, a harsh, rhythmic thudding drew our attention.

We stopped dead in our tracks.

Stew looked at Bean. I looked at Bean. Bean looked at Stew and then at me. We all nodded.

The sound pounded through the unlit blackness.

'Why did you nod?' Stew asked me, in a slightly faster-than-was-necessary whisper.

'Because you and Bean both did,' I whispered back.

'No, you nodded first,' Bean said to me, attempting to assert some form of leadership by talking slightly more slowly and loudly than either Stew or myself.

'No, I didn't,' I countered. 'I only nodded because you two did. Why else would I nod?'

'Maybe you nodded because of the noise,' Stew said.

'I wasn't head banging,' I said. 'I didn't suddenly confuse being here with being at Glastonbury. I was nodding in agreement, not moving to the rhythm.'

'What were you agreeing with?' Bean asked.

'I've got no idea.'

'You can't agree with something you've got no idea about.'

'Then maybe it was a knee-jerk reaction,' I said. 'Maybe it was an involuntary thing, like when someone beeps their horn as they drive past, and you automatically wave your hand even though you haven't seen who it is.'

'For that to be the case, someone else would have to have nodded first,' Stew said. 'You can't nod as a knee-jerk reaction, unless you're responding to an initial stimulus.'

'But that's what I was doing.' My whisper was in danger of slithering into a shout. I forced myself to hold back. 'I nodded because you two did.'

We all fell silent again, each of us taking personal responsibility for getting off the roundabout we had just created.

The thudding increased in tempo.

'It's coming from over there,' Stew said, pointing to one o'clock.

'No,' I said. 'It's definitely coming from over there.' I pointed to fifteen minutes past the hour.

'C'mon, then.' Bean started walking. Stew and I followed suit.

'Where are we going?' Stew asked.

'We're going to split the difference,' Bean said. 'We'll go to seven-and-a-half minutes past and work it out from there.'

'And what do we do if it's Barry, and he's all psyched up?'

I took out my mobile phone. 'You two make lots of noise. Really aggressive, threatening noise, and I call nine-nine-nine.'

'Good idea.' Bean nodded.

I resisted the temptation to nod back.

'Make it clear to him,' Bean said, 'that you're calling the police. Let him know that the professionals are going to be rushing over here in full force.'

'Do you think he'll surrender?' Stew asked.

'I expect that he'll run,' Bean replied. 'Wouldn't you?'

'I certainly wouldn't try to Boom-Ka-Ka-Chow my way out of here,' I said.

Stew ignored me. 'I hope he doesn't have a knife,' he said.

'I hope we save a girl's life,' I said, forcing myself to peer into the darkness. 'That is why we're here.'

The thudding was louder now. It was no faster, but it was definitely louder. And it was coming from a place that was undeniably closer to a quarter past the hour.

My silent self-congratulation was cut short by the sudden sound of a woman's voice.

'Oh, my God!'

The thudding quickened and then stopped abruptly.

We all moved instinctively in her direction.

Half-a-dozen paces and we were suddenly there, closer than we wanted to be.

175

The woman was bent over the bonnet of the car. Her short skirt was up over her hips. Her face was towards us. Her eyes were closed. The man's trousers had puddled around his ankles. His hands were on the woman's hips.

They had no idea we were present. They were both lost in their own world. I felt like we had just broken into their home. I looked at the boys. They were both looking up at the sky.

I waved at them to get their attention. Then I pointed to our left. They both nodded. We moved away without disturbing the car-coupling.

3.

We left even more quickly than we'd arrived.

Stew kept glancing over his shoulder as I led the way towards the other side of the park.

'We're not being followed,' Stew whispered.

'You don't have to be quiet now,' I said. 'The couple didn't know we saw them and wouldn't chase us if they had.'

'How do you know?'

'Because they were doing what was best for them, not what they thought we needed.'

'Fair point.'

After a couple of minutes, Bean stopped walking.

'Why have we stopped here?' Stew asked before I could.

'It's as good as anywhere else.' Bean made a point of looking in every direction. 'We have to pause and take stock, so we might as well do it here.'

I couldn't argue with that.

'That was the worst thing ever.' Stew said. 'Did you see what they had on their fingers?'

'I dread to think,' Bean said.

Stew ignored him. 'They were wearing wedding rings,' he said. 'The pair of them. They were married.'

'Not necessarily to each other,' Bean pointed out.

'Which is the worst option?' Stew pointed a finger as he spoke. His raised hand seemed wet-as-dishwater compared to Wee Drop's. 'Which is worse?' he asked again. 'They're married and they're happy to do that in public. Or they're married to other people, and they're doing this on the quiet?'

'They weren't so quiet,' I said. 'We probably wouldn't have found them if they had been.'

'I wish we hadn't,' Stew wiped his hands together. 'They were like animals.'

'Worse than,' I said. 'Pigeons are monogamous. A male pigeon actually courts the female, there are genuine rituals involved, and if she agrees they mate for life.'

Stew frowned. 'Aren't rituals the sole preserve of the human species?'

'Humans came late to that party. Birds had rituals long before people did; birds and the rest of nature.'

'That's an interesting thesis.'

'It's a fact, not a thesis.'

'Anyway,' Bean brought us back to what he needed to talk about. 'Let's forget pigeons for a while, shall we? There's still a lot of the park we haven't checked out.'

'We can't do it all in one night,' Stew said. 'And if there were other people around, they'd probably have been over there, too.' He gestured vaguely in the direction of the couple and their car.

'What do you think, Jack?' Bean offered me the casting vote.

It didn't seem like a good time to take sides. 'I think we can do a bit of both,' I said. 'We can make our way to the Angel Road entrance, which, by my reckoning, is a few hundred yards in that direction,' I pointed straight ahead, 'and we can check out that area of the park as we go. What do you say?'

Stew was almost convinced. 'Are you sure the Angel Road gates are open this time of night?'

'They're never locked,' I said.

'How do you know?'

I didn't know. I was guessing.

'It's just one of those things,' I said, as convincingly as I could.

'Ok,' Stew said. 'Let's go.'

Bean took the lead without saying a word. I patted Stew on his shoulder, and we set off together.

We'd gone barely a hundred yards when we heard Barry's voice.

We all turned and looked at the same time. Although we couldn't see him, the landlord was somewhere to our right, in a small patch of woodland. I heard Bean sigh. I felt Stew tense. For the first time in my life, I'd gone out of my way to make something happen that I didn't want to happen, and it was happening now.

Bean kept his eyes on the woodland as he spoke. 'Let's go boys.'

Somehow, despite my fear, a part of me wanted to say what a clichéd line that was.

Thankfully, my mouth was suddenly not in good working order.

We walked in silence into the woodland and towards the voice.

4.

Barry was standing in a small clearing, with his back to us. He was facing a young, dark-haired woman, who was leaning against a tree. She saw us as we approached.

'Oh my God – look!' She pointed as she spoke.

The landlord spun round.

'Evening, Barry.'

Admittedly, it wasn't the best opening line when you were on the verge of making a citizen's arrest, but you've got to start somewhere, and I hadn't prepared a script. Regardless, it made Barry pull a face – a mix of anger and fear – and raise both his hands.

'What the hell?' He glared at the three of us. 'So this is what you all do when you've finished drinking? I knew it! You're a bunch of perverts!'

'We are?' Stew was the loudest he'd been all night. 'You're calling us perverts when you're the one getting ready to kill another of the working girls!'

'What are you talking about? I don't kill prostitutes! I've never killed anyone!' Barry's hands tightened into fists.

'Don't lie! You're only one kill away from changing category!' Stew raised his wet dishcloth finger. 'If we hadn't got here when we did, this poor thing,' Stew jabbed his w-d-f towards the girl, 'would have been the one that turned you from spree into serial.'

'What?'

'There's a psycho killing working girls,' I said.

'And you fit the profile!' Stew shouted.

Barry's eyes widened. 'What profile?'

'The profile of the guy who's killing the girls,' I said.

'But I've already told you, I'm not a killer! I'm the opposite! I'm the guy who...who...' His voice trailed off. His shoulders slumped.

The young woman stepped forwards, patting one of his fists as she did so.

She studied the three of us briefly. There was something in her eyes that reminded me of Bella. And there was something else. Something about her face. What was it I'd said to Morgan?

Much older than my years.

That was it. I hadn't mean it. Not quite, anyway. But it was certainly true for this girl.

Much older than her years.

Maybe there was a fast lane in the motorway of life? Maybe sometimes the hard shoulder of society forced a person into it, and kept them there until their death came cold and fast?

I felt an overwhelming urge to offer this girl hope. Even if it was false.

'It will turn into Spaghetti Junction,' I said. 'You need to believe that.'

'What does that mean?' She seemed inquisitive and distant at the same time.

'It means that just because it seems like a straight road from Nottingham to Leicester, it really isn't.'

'I like Leicester,' the girl said. 'I go there sometimes, just to take a break.'

For the second time that night, I felt tears in my eyes.

5.

It took us only ten more minutes to accept the truth.

It was as sad, tragic, and heart-warming as only truth in a complex world can be.

The young woman explained that, far from being a threat to the working girls, Barry had appointed himself their informal protector. Since the first lockdown, he had walked around late at night, getting to know them, making sure they were safe. Sometimes, he even gave a girl money on condition that she went straight home. All he had asked in return, was that they told no one of his activity.

'We all know what happened to Bella,' the young woman said. 'And, since then, Barry has been out here whenever he can. He can't keep us all safe, obviously. But it's good to know someone cares.'

I looked at the young woman. She looked back. She wasn't inquisitive anymore. She felt even more distant. I couldn't think of a question that would reach her.

Barry had a question, though. 'Who told you that I was the killer?'

Bean and Stu both looked to me for the answer.

'It's not really that simple,' I began. 'No one gave us your name, no one pointed the finger, as it were. It's more that we misinterpreted a clue,' I stared pointedly at Bean.

'What clue was that?' Barry moved a step in my direction. His voice had hardened. His shoulders were no longer slumped. I glanced around in the hope that Wee Drop and the Fish had suddenly appeared. They hadn't.

'It was, erm...'

'It was the fact that you were out here night after night.' Bean came to my defence. 'As you'd expect, we can't reveal who told us that, but it was shared in good faith. You're not the only one who thinks that the girls need protection and that the killer should be caught.'

'And, unfortunately, you do fit the profile of a serial killer,' Stu added.

Barry turned away from me. 'Which serial killer?' He asked Stu.

My fellow-quizzer blinked. 'Which serial killer, what?'

'Which serial killer do I fit the profile of? Which one am I supposed to be like?'

'It's not a specific profile.' It was my turn to intercede. The few seconds break had been all I needed to regroup. 'You're not like Ted Bundy's twin, or Harold Shipman's sibling. You just match some generic features – gender, age, that sort of thing.'

Barry shook his head. 'And that's it? You thought I was a serial killer because I'm a white man of a certain age?'

'Your skin colour wasn't really that relevant,' Stu shrugged apologetically. 'To be fair, it does all seem a bit thin, now.'

'You reckon?'

'Sorry.'

We all apologised to Barry. He didn't reply. Instead, he turned away from us, gave the young woman a twenty-pound note and said that he was sorry she had been caught up in this. I gave her an additional tenner, just because.

Barry then made a point of looking at his watch and telling everyone he was going home. We all mumbled 'Good night' and he walked past us as if we weren't there.

The young woman said nothing and set off across the park without so-much as a backward glance.

The three of us had no points left to make. Truth be told, it felt as if we hadn't made any worthwhile points in the first place. So far, our evening's work had been pointless. I was suddenly aware that the ground felt cold and hard beneath my trainers.

Bean broke the silence that had slipped in like an uninvited guest.

'I hope Morgan's behind the bar tomorrow, and not him.'

'Yeah,' Stu scratched his scalp. 'Where we are concerned, Barry's service quality is going to drop even lower.'

At which point, my mobile phone started ringing.

I stared at the caller ID.

'Who is it?' Bean asked.

'The Paddington Fish.'

'Well, answer it then.'

I did. My hands were suddenly shaking and cold. My toes were numb. I felt as if the real me – Jack Morgan - was trapped somewhere in-between my extremities.

'Fish, how are you? What's happening? What's the news?' I forced myself to shut up. I'd much sooner have kept asking the same question in a hundred different ways, than listen to his answer. I was sure it wasn't going to be good.

'It's Wee Drop,' the Fish said.

The phone went silent. I couldn't hear a thing. I couldn't even hear him breathing. I wondered if he had collapsed. Then I remembered it was the Fish, and he barely breathed anyway.

'What's happened to Wee Drop?' I asked.

Bean and Stew automatically moved a step closer to each other.

'He's had an accident,' the Fish said. 'He was on his own on one side of Burrow Avenue. Thoughtless and me were on the other. Turned out there were some minor road works being done and someone – kids presumably – had hidden the signs. Wee Drop fell down the hole.'

'Oh my God! How bad is it?'

'We had to get an ambulance. I'm at the hospital with him now.'

'We'll come right over! It's only a fifteen-minute walk from where we are.'

'Roger that.' The Fish hung up.

I shared the news with Bean and Stew.

We set off as fast as we were able.

6.

We arrived twenty-five minutes later.[23]

The Fish was sitting motionless in Accident and Emergency. The drunks, druggies, hypochondriacs, pensioners, terrified first-time parents, and teenagers who were just beginning to appreciate that they weren't invulnerable, all seemed oblivious to his presence.

He didn't move when we approached him.

This time I got straight to the point.

'How is he?'

'Don't know. Still waiting.' The Fish glanced sideways as Bean collapsed into the chair next to him.

'How far did he fall?' Stew asked perhaps the most important question.

'Not far. It wasn't a deep hole. Only eight or ten inches. The problem was he didn't see it coming.'

'He probably tensed as he fell.'

'It sounded like it. He hit with a thud, and he yelled really loud. Thoughtless and me had to help him out of the hole because he couldn't take any weight on his ankles.'

'Where is Thoughtless?' I double-checked the waiting room just in case our yoga expert was doing some crazy animal stretch on the floor.

'Stayed out looking for Barry; going to call me if necessary. It seemed the best use of our resources. Wee Drop doesn't need two of us sitting here.'

'You're right,' I said. 'We'd have taken the same approach, only we found Barry and he isn't our man.'

The Fish straightened. 'How do you know?'

'We had words with him. His story checked out. We'd

---

[23] Bean's not the fastest.

184

just decided to pack it in for the night when you called.'

'That means we don't have a suspect anymore.'

'That's right.'

'What are we going to do now? I liked it when we had a suspect.'

'We'll get another one.'

'I hope so.'

For the first time ever, I saw a glimmer of fragility in the Paddington Fish. I found it both heart-warming and disconcerting. I slipped into reassuring-mode.

'We will uncover another suspect. Really quickly. I guarantee it.'

I felt like a parent promising a child that we'd get a new hamster just as soon as we'd buried the recently demised, and much loved, Toothy, who'd made the fatal mistake of going one revolution too far, too fast.

Behind us, a skin-and-bone, tattooed, twenty-something with a violent green Mohican and red blotches on his face and scalp, began telling everyone in the room that he was the last of his kind, and was going to kill us all.

I checked automatically for any sign of tomahawks. Fish just turned slowly and stared at him. The fragility of a moment ago disappeared deep below the surface. Skin-and-bone stopped talking and began picking at his fingernails. I wanted to tell him it was easier to stare at your shoes, but I decided against it. I figured he had the right to live or die by his own choices.

To Bean's left, an eighty-something was trying to persuade his wife that it had only been a touch of heartburn after all, and they'd both be better off tucked up in bed. She wasn't having any of it. Fear of losing her fella was clearly overriding her fear of this place and the loud mishmash of people it contained.

'A real motley crew,' Stew whispered, too quietly for

Bean to hear.

'Yeah. I'd sooner be an out-of-breath, time-limited hamster pushing my luck on the wheel of fortune, than a nurse in here.'

'A hamster?'

'It doesn't matter.'

'You need to tell Thoughtless to stop looking and go home,' Bean said suddenly. 'We should always have back-up when we're out searching. We need to make that a rule. I think we should plan to regroup tomorrow, midday, in the pub and agree to that.'

'Good idea.'

I walked back towards the entrance, took out my phone, and called Thoughtless's number. It rang seven times and then went to answerphone. I tried again. And a third time. I was forced to leave a voicemail.

I'm rubbish at voicemails. I usually say something that's completely unnecessary, go on for too long and get cut off. I even waste time introducing myself, even when calling friends, even though I know that my name and number will have already appeared on their phone. Not only that, I waste even more time telling them what time it is.

That's the equivalent of walking up to the next-door-neighbour you've known for decades and saying, 'Hi, I'm Jack and it's now seven minutes past eleven,' before beginning the conversation. And doing that every time you meet them.

To make matters worse, something happens to my voice when I leave a voicemail. My breathing changes and I speak faster, with a higher pitch, and I add a slight, but very noticeable, posh note. I end up sounding like a BBC News at Six presenter who's just rushed into the studio and hasn't quite got their breath back before announcing that a businessman selling ninety-degree angles has cornered the market.

One of the great things about communicating with Shades is that technology can't get in the way.

I love the fact that the afterlife is a mobile phone free zone. You can't take selfies. You're no longer proud of the warp-speed processing you possess. You can no longer send self-indulgent messages telling everyone you're having a bad day because a cloud formation has just reminded you of your Grandad, who died in his allotment whilst trying to pull out a particularly deep-rooted pumpkin.

Technology may be shaping our future, but only up to the full-stop at the end of this particular life sentence. There are other sentences that follow - paragraphs, pages, books, libraries, even, I don't know – that are shaped by the universal, rather than the world-wide, web.

I just hope that the eternal spider creating and connecting it all never requires me to leave a next-life version of a voicemail. Or if they do, I hope that the next-life version of me can handle it a lot better.

By the time I'd stopped imagining a spiritual Theraphosa blondi as the ultimate cause of everything, a doctor had started talking to the boys. They were all on their feet. I pocketed my phone and hurried over.

'Hi, I'm Jack,' I said, cutting the doctor off mid-sentence.

He turned and stared at me. The others glared. I looked at the wall clock. The self-destructive part of me wanted to tell them what time it was.

Bean came to everyone's rescue.

'The doctor was just telling us that Wee Drop has broken his right ankle and severely bruised his left. He's going to be leaving here in a wheelchair.'

'Ouch!'

187

'Ouch, indeed.'

'But he will be able to walk again?' I looked at the doctor. I guessed he was in his mid-thirties. He had short, brown hair and a very straight back. If he was carrying any fat on his body, it was well hidden. He was wearing black Michael Caine-from-the-sixties glasses. Although he was standing within arm's reach, something about his manner made me feel that we were on opposite sides of the Grand Canyon.

I remembered the young woman in the park, and wondered for the first time what her name was.

'There's no reason to think that he won't,' the doctor said.

'So there's every reason to think that he will?' I said.

'I just said that.'

'You said it in a negative way.'

'Two negatives make a positive,' the doctor said.

'That's true,' Stew said. 'In Mathematics, every number has what's known as an "additive inverse", which, when added to the original number, always results in a score of zero. Two negatives make a positive because the inverse of the inverse of a positive number is the same positive number.'

I looked again at the wall clock. I don't think the hands had moved.

'I'm going to wait here for Wee Drop to be released,' the Paddington Fish said. 'Then I'm going to see him home and make sure everything's alright. I'll be in the pub for midday.' He cocked his head to one side. 'Did you manage to speak to Thoughtless?'

'No. I left a voicemail.'

'Then we've done all we can,' Bean said. 'Let's call it a night.'

'I've still got work to do,' the doctor said. He walked

away without saying another word.

'Do you think he's related to that RSPCA Inspector?' I asked.

No one answered.

The Fish sat down again. He might as well have gone to the bottom of the deep end. We all knew better than to follow.

Bean checked his pockets – for what, I don't know – and set off towards the doors.

Team Alpha left in silence.

It seemed the best way to go.

7.

We separated after a few streets.

I found myself appreciating the chance to be alone.

Sometimes there's nothing I like more. Sometimes it's the worst thing in the world. The difference between the two is simple: it's me. It's how I am and what I bring to, or what I let grow in, the empty space.

Loneliness is not the absence of people, it's a state of mind. How you feel whenever you are alone is determined by how you manage your mind-space, by how well you control your memories and your imagination.

I can feel lonely when there are other people around.

Conversely, I can feel comforted and secure when there's no one.

When I get it completely wrong, the Black Hole expands to fill every available space – inside and out – and then it sucks me in like the vacuum cleaner from Hell.

If you've never been inside a vacuum cleaner, you're a lucky bunny. It's a horrible place to be. It's loud and irresistible. You're pulled ever deeper, swirling around, with stuff getting in your eyes and clogging your nose and throat. You want to rip your skin open, just to give it all a way out. You want to shout for help, but stuff gets in as soon as you try. You don't know which way is up. You can't find your footing. You can't remember how things used to be. There is no help. You have no hope. You're there because you deserve to be. You're there because you're rubbish.

Now, though, walking back to 5a, the vacuum cleaner was unplugged. Somehow, after the third most challenging day of my adult life, these few moments alone were serving as a much-needed comfort-blanket. [24]

The last person I expected to see – and very definitely the last person I wanted to see – was Barry.

He was standing, with his back against a wall, just a couple of hundred yards from my home. He was waiting for me.

A voice in my mind said,

'What if you made a terrible mistake earlier and he really is the p-n-j? What if he's going to break his pattern and cover his tracks by killing the three of you tonight? What if you're about to be stabbed to death?'

I heard the click of a switch as the vacuum cleaner was plugged in. I felt the delicate, but unmistakable, clinginess of a spider's web around my eyes. Because my feet are hateful, with minds of their own, they kept walking towards the landlord.

'You don't have to do this,' my mouth said.

My feet took no notice.

---

[24] The two most challenging days in my life were when Ricky disappeared under a bus, and when my parents died, together, in a car accident. A double-decker took my brother. An HGV smashed through my Mum and Dad's Volvo. That's why I only go out on my scooter when I have no other choice.

Barry pushed himself away from the wall and blocked my path.

My mouth tried again.

'There's still time to turn round.'

Fear coated the words. Fear, sticky as treacle, began clogging my insides, tightening my stomach. Making my heart work harder.

'I've never liked treacle.'

'What'd you say?' Barry had his hands open, in front of his chest. His feet owned the pavement. He looked bigger than I'd ever seen him. 'What'd you say?' He repeated.

'Treacle,' I said, tasting it on my lips and feeling it thicken my tongue. 'I've never liked it.'

My feet stopped just in time. We were about two paces apart.

'You do talk some rubbish,' Barry said.

'I know.'

'The only time you're not talking rubbish is when you're quizzing.' He considered briefly. 'And when you're talking to Morgan.'

'I know.'

'You were talking rubbish tonight, about me.'

'I know that, too.'

'You could ruin a man, talking that sort of rubbish about him. You could take away everything he's got.'

'Yes.'

Barry took a step to towards me. My feet chose to stay where they were. The rest of me questioned that decision. The rest of me tried to pick up my right foot and force it backwards. My foot was having none of it. I felt like a rabbit in the headlights in the fast lane; I was suddenly much closer to Leicester than I wanted to be.

'The thing is,' Barry lowered his voice. 'How do I know that I can trust you?'

191

'What...What do you mean?' The treacle was making talking tricky. My survival instinct urged me to keep my mouth working. 'Just tell me what you're talking about, and I'll give you the very best answer I can.'

'I don't want you to conjure up the best answer, I want the truth. Cast iron.' Barry licked his lips.

I wished that I could do the same.[25] But it was taking everything I'd got just to manage some words.

'I can do cast iron.' I forced those out and it felt as if some of the stickiness went with them.

'Right.' Barry inched closer. 'We made a deal back there, in the park. But I've been thinking about it, and it's clear to me that I'm the only one whose life will be ruined if the deal's not honoured. Everyone knows you three are losers, so if it turned out you'd been skulking around spying on people, no one would be surprised. But I'm one of the pillars of the community and if, well, if stuff came out about me, there'd be those who wouldn't believe I was trying to look after the girls. There are some who'd be happy to believe something bad about me. I could lose my reputation and the pub. I can't afford that.'

'We gave you our word, you heard us.' I sensed that my mouth was suddenly on a roll, so I kept out of the way. 'We only ever do that when we're being serious. I promise you we'll say nothing. We're good at saying nothing.'

'The three of you are only ever serious when you're quizzing.'

'That's the only time you see us being serious. We're more than just quizzers. Just like you're more than just a landlord. You can't judge us on that one thing.'

'You judged me on a profile that wasn't specific.'

---

[25] Lick my lips, not Barry's.

192

'And we were wrong to do so. That's my point. That's what we've acknowledged, and why you can trust us to keep silent from now on.'

Barry lowered his hands for the first time since we had started talking. He licked his lips again. I managed to lick mine. Although my feet still weren't under my control, the fact that my mouth was, felt like an important step in the right direction.

'The thing is,' Barry said quietly, 'I've spent my life hiding.'

I felt like I'd been punched in the chest. I gasped and clutched momentarily at my heart.

'You're not alone!' My words gushed. 'I'm always hiding too. So are my friends. We're all hiding.'

'I thought I was the only one.'

'We've all got our own reasons.'

'I can't afford to be found out.'

'You won't be.' I felt my feet come back under my control. I inched them forwards. 'We're on the same side now, so we won't ever say anything, and no one else will ever look at you that closely. That's our safety net. Think about it. People don't look, not really. They glance at us like they glance at headlines. Until right now that always annoyed me. Thing is, you've just made me accept that, when we're choosing to hide, we can't blame people for not seeing us. Instead, we should be grateful for the fact that their lives blind them.'

'Jesus...' Barry stared past me into the night. '...You're right. You can be serious when you're not quizzing.'

'Only when the planets align. If Telescopium and Microscopium are not magnifying fully, I'm no use to anyone.'

'What?'

'Nothing.'

193

Barry was silent for a little longer than I was comfortable with. Then he offered his right hand. I shook it.

'I feel safe again,' he said.

'Good. I'm glad.'

We released each other's hand. We both almost smiled. We chose instead to hide.

We went our separate ways without saying another word.

I felt that 5a was calling me.

8.

Darius was alone.

That was enough to put my heart back into overdrive.

'Where are the girls?'

'I don't know. They went out.'

'When did they go? Where did they say they were going? What did they say they were going to do?'

Darius recoiled. I couldn't blame him. My mouth was rushing out questions.

'Bella must have said something! What did she say?'

'She said they, er, they were, er...'

'All you have to do is remember what she told you!'

'I'm sorry,' Darius backed away. 'I'm trying to get it absolutely right, and you keep asking more.'

'I'm sorry. It's been an emotional search.' I scratched my head. 'It's been a long night – it's been a long, long, day – and all we've got to show for it are two damaged ankles and a landlord who isn't a p-n-j.'

'You confronted Barry?'

'Yeah. He's no more a psycho-nut-job than I'm Jacob Rees-Mogg.'

'That's a shame.'

'Which is?'

'Both. It would have been good if Barry had been your guy and you'd caught him, and there are a few things I'd like to have said to Jacob Rees-Mogg.'

'There'd be a queue.'

'Patience was one of my things. I was good at waiting.'

'What were you waiting for?'

'It varied. When I was feeling down, I hoped for something more than just books. On my good days, "I said to my soul, be still, and wait without hope, for hope would be hope for the wrong thing."'

'Did you tell yourself that because you believed it, or because Eliot wrote it?'

'I wanted to believe it."

'And now?'

'I remember hope like I remember coffee.' For the briefest moment, Darius softened around his edges. Then the lines filled in again. 'Who damaged their ankles?'

'Wee Drop. He fell into a hole.'

'How is he?'

'Wheelchair-bound, with the Paddington Fish looking after him.'

'And what happened to you?'

'What do you mean?'

'You look different.'

'Oh. I, erm...' It was my turn to hesitate. 'I, erm...I don't know, somewhere, despite all the madness – maybe because of it – somewhere, I realised something.'

'Was it an add-on realisation or a let-go realisation?'

'What?'

'There are only two types.'

'Can't it be a bit of both?'

'It's your realisation.'

'Yeah.'

I tried to find the answer to Darius's question. Add-on or let-go? It was a most basic 50-50. It should have been easy, but I felt like I was standing on the hyphen between the two fifties; swaying from side-to-side, struggling to keep my balance as it swung between the numbers.

'Why not just tell me about it?' Darius suggested. 'Maybe that will give you a clue as to what type it is.'

'Good call.'

I brought my hands together and straightened my back. My eyes asked for permission to stare at my shoes. It wasn't granted. My eyes made it clear they didn't know where else to look. I directed them at Darius. He seemed more than Ok with that.

I didn't get chance to open my mouth. I didn't get close to saying a word.

Bella and Doreen burst into 5a and took my breath away.

'You've let him do it again! How could you?' Bella's voice was barely recognisable. 'How could you let him kill again?' She didn't wait for an answer. She just needed to release. She couldn't stop herself from releasing. 'There were six of you and you still couldn't stop him! And it was worse this time! Do you understand? It was worse!'

Bella screamed. Doreen wailed. Darius staggered backwards.

I didn't have an answer. There wasn't an answer that would have done anything other than stoke the flames. The question I had was no better.

'Did you know her – the working girl he killed?'

Bella's scream turned into a roar, a mix of anger and pain coming from deep inside. It felt like being hit by a tidal wave. My mind swirled. The room spun. Bella roared a second time. I was vaguely aware of Doreen spinning towards Darius. I grabbed hold of the back of a chair.

196

The roar echoed.

It took all of Bella's energy with it. She doubled over. If she'd been alive, she would have thrown up.

When she finally straightened, she said, 'It wasn't one of us. Not this time. Not tonight. He changed it tonight. He changed it.'

'What – he killed a man?'

'No. He killed a woman, just not a working girl.'

'How...How do you know?'

Bella shook her head. She glanced at Doreen. She got a brief nod of support. She forced herself to look me full in the face. I barely recognised her light-blues.

'Because I know the woman,' Bella said. 'We all do.'

'What? Who?'

Bella didn't blink. Her expression hardened.

'He killed Thoughtless,' she said.

9.

Sometimes tidal waves are silent and invisible. Sometimes they knock you down, throw you back, then pull you all the way to the horizon where the Black Hole is waiting.

As I tumbled and crashed towards oblivion, I felt Bella's presence reach like a net into the tempest. I felt her draw me in and pull me out. I felt my feet gripping the floor, my fingers gripping the chair. The room tried to roll from side to side like a boat in a storm.

Bella calmed even that. Once again, her emotional outburst had transformed into concern for me.

'I was so scared to come home,' she said. 'I'm so angry and so scared, so scared for you. I knew how you'd be, and I didn't know if I could catch you. Not tonight.'

'You caught me.'

'What shall I do now?'

'Keep me on dry land, away from…You know.'

'Yes.'

'Keep me safe while you tell me what's happened. Tell me everything.'

'Are you sure?'

'I don't have a choice.'

'I understand.'

Bella told me. I listened. Throughout I imagined that I was standing, facing the shoreline rather than the horizon. I imagined Bella as my lighthouse, guiding me in safely. Even then, it was the worst of journeys.

Bella had decided that she and Doreen would form a third team searching for Barry. She had instructed Darius to stay behind. The girls followed their own route. Eventually, they'd arrived at the Arboretum. The gates were locked by the time they got there. That made no difference to the Shades, or to the working girls who knew other ways in.

'It's one of those spots some girls really like to use,' Bella said. 'I never did, but some thought it was the best place. If you knew your way around, it was easy to find somewhere private.'

Bella's report continued and I stared ahead, silent, and defenceless.

They had found Thoughtless, mutilated, and naked, in the pond. Her face was being rained on by the fountain. Someone had dragged her there and positioned her, with her wounds on show. The water was bloody. Her long brown hair was stained and matted. Her eyes were open. Two of her fingers were broken, pointing up at the stars.

'He didn't tie her up,' Bella said. 'Don't you understand? He could have knocked her out then tied her, but he chose not to.' Bella hardened slightly. 'The only possible reason he didn't tie her up, is because he wanted a struggle. He wanted to give her the chance to fight for her life. He wanted a scrap.'

'Thoughtless would still be alive if I hadn't asked her to help,' I said.

'She'd have still been alive if I hadn't forced you into helping us!' The hard edge strengthened. 'But I did, and you did, and she said "Yes". We're not the guilty ones here, Barry is. He's the one who's got to pay for what's happened!'

'It isn't Barry.'

'What do you mean?'

I shrugged.

Darius filled in the gap. 'They found Barry while they were out. He's not the killer.'

'For sure?'

'For sure. The truth is, we don't have a suspect,' I said dully. 'And I don't know where to look. Even though I promised the Fish, I don't know where to look. And the universe keeps expanding.' A question stabbed through my mind. 'Where's Thoughtless now? Where's her body?'

'She's - It's in the fountain,' Bella corrected herself deliberately. 'The best bet now is that they'll come across it when they unlock the gates.'

Another question stabbed, this one offered the pain of hope, a remission of sorts. 'Did you see...her? Was she there when you were at the fountain?'

'Her Shade?'

'Yes. Is her Shade outside, waiting to come in?'

'No.' Bella was expressionless. 'Her Shade was long gone.'

'How could you tell? What if she was there and you missed her?'

'She'd have made herself known. Or we would have

seen her, or sensed her, or something, just like you did with Darius.'

'But I'm the psychic medium, here. Not you.'

'No. We're Shades. We know our own. She wasn't there.'

There was a finality in the way Bella spoke that stopped me pushing the point.

'Then, she's homeless?'

It was Bella's turn to shrug.

'If she isn't here,' I said, 'It means she's either homeless and lonely, or that she didn't fall out of the rollercoaster.'

'You mean she could have already gone through the door?' Darius said. 'She could already be ahead of us?'

'Wow!' Doreen span round in a tight circle. 'Imagine that!'

'I can't,' Bella said coldly.

'What do you think the chances are?' Darius asked me. 'You know, that she stayed on the rollercoaster to the end of the ride?'

'Honestly, I have no idea.' It was hard to engage with Darius's question.

'There is a third option,' Bella said. 'Thoughtless could have fallen out, just like we all did, and met another psychic medium. She could be in a different version of 5a.'

'As far as I know,' I said, 'I'm the only psychic medium alive. And if I'm not, there aren't many others. The odds are stacked against Thoughtless bumping into one.'

'How do you know?' Bella frowned. 'Just how do you know there are so few psychic mediums? Eh?'

I didn't offer an answer. Bella paused just long enough to make me acknowledge that I didn't have an answer.

'You hide yourself away, so why wouldn't they? How do you know there aren't a dozen others within a mile of this house, all hiding away, all thinking they're unique?

How do you know that isn't true?'

'You're right, I don't.'

Bella wasn't listening. She hadn't finished talking yet. 'For all you know, there might be an official list of psychic medium accommodation available to Shades, that us three missed, and you're not on. For all you know, you're the only medium running unregistered premises in the city!'

'Hadn't thought of that,' Doreen admitted. 'Still, I wouldn't want to have gone anywhere else.'

'Neither would I,' Darius said. 'If Thoughtless did fall off, like we did, I hope she bumps into someone as nice as you. That's all any Shade can ask for.'

10.

For too long, I've only ever focused on the bad things that can happen. These days, whenever I consider the future, I'm drawn immediately to expect the worst of all possibilities.

I don't know if my mind does this because I've been in the Black Hole, or if I've been in the Black Hole because my mind does this. Either way, I'm not so much a glass-half-empty type of guy, as a glass-will-soon-be-broken-and-on-the-floor-cutting-into-your-feet type of guy.

Most days, the thought that there might be a dozen genuine psychic mediums within walking distance of 5a, would have had me sulking uncontrollably.

This wasn't most days.

This wasn't like any other day ever.

That's the only reason I've got for what my mind did next.

It didn't give me chance to get in the way. Instead, it flashed an insight, bright as a sky-high neon sign, that dominated my senses.

'Damn it!' I stepped away from the chair. 'I've had the answer wrong from the very beginning.'

'What answer?' It was Darius who asked.

'The answer to the crucial conundrum.'

'But dat droll hen does translate as *the landlord*. That's not wrong.'

'What was wrong was treating it as a conundrum in the first place. I only did that because I'm an obsessive quizzer who answers questions and doesn't ask them. If I did, I would have questioned my immediate interpretation. I would have asked myself why it had to be a conundrum. I would have explored alternatives. As it was, I just settled for the first answer I came up with and ran with that. I saw what I expected to. I decided it was right and led us all in a vicious circle.'

'Then what does dat droll hen mean?'

'It doesn't mean anything. It isn't code. It isn't a clue. It's a straightforward identification. It is what it is, and nothing more. I made it something more by being an arrogant fool.' I glanced at Bella. 'All I had to do was take it literally. The answer wasn't hidden in plain sight because it wasn't even hidden. It was there, right in front of my eyes, and I didn't know how to see it.'

'We've got the point,' Bella stopped me talking. 'You got it wrong. We've all made mistakes. Now that you've recognised yours, get over yourself and tell us who dat droll hen identifies.'

I didn't know if I wanted to shout at my Shade-sister or hug her. If I'd been able to hold her, I'd have probably done both.

'It's Morgan,' I said. 'She's the droll hen.'

11.

Bella fell silent. Darius watched me. Doreen asked the question.

'How does that work?'

'Morgan was engaged to be married. She was planning her hen party.'

'And she's got that humorous style?' Darius focused on the other part of the phrase. 'You're sure of that?'

'All day long.'

'What style are you talking about?' It was Doreen's turn again.

'Her sense of humour. She's droll.'

'I don't know what that means,' Doreen said. 'You're either funny or you're not, aren't you?'

'Ultimately, yes.'

Doreen tutted. 'I bet it was men who came up with all the different styles.'

Before I could reply Bella asked, 'If Morgan is dat droll hen, does that mean she's connected to the killer or that she's a future victim?'

'I don't know.' Black and white images of Thoughtless, unmoving, and dead, redirected my thoughts, draining them into a pond, viscous and shadowed despite the fountain.

'Then you need to go and find out.' Bella was back into full-on dog-with-a-bone. 'Whichever it is, there isn't time to waste. Women are at risk, and there's no telling what he'll do to his next victim.'

Doreen glanced down at her body. I hoped she had no black and white images of her own.

'If you've got her number on your phone, you need to call her now,' Bella went on. 'One way or another, she provides a direct route to the killer.'

I made the call. It rang straight through to her answerphone. I hung up.

'She didn't reply,' I said. 'There's no way I'm leaving a message.'

'Try again,' Bella said.

I did. I got the same result.

'Do you know where she lives?'

I nodded.

'Get there now. How long will it take?'

'It's a twenty-minute walk.'

'Take the scooter.'

'I've not driven that for a while.'

'You can manage it, though. Right?' Bella didn't wait for my reply. 'Drive fast and safe. You need to get there in one piece.'

As ever, there was only one right answer. 'Yes.'

'Shouldn't Jack contact the others? Shouldn't he take them with him?' Darius was obviously worried.

'He can't take a team on his scooter,' Bella said. 'The others don't have a car between them, and we don't have time to waste. No, Jack needs to get to Morgan now, as fast as he can.'

'Bella's right,' I said. 'We don't always agree, but this time we do.'

She didn't respond. I didn't look at her. She ignored me. I ignored her. Truth be told, neither of us was ignoring the other. We didn't do goodbyes. We'd never really done hello. We'd both pretended that our time together had just happened without it having anything to do with either of us. We'd both pretended that it wasn't a big deal.

It had, of course, turned into the biggest deal. We both knew that. Occasionally one of us even said something to that effect, secure in the knowledge that the other would pretend not to hear. We were good at pretending with each other. Right now, we needed to be.

I put on a jacket and a scarf and a pair of black, leather gloves. I got my helmet and the key for my blue 1986 Vespa Douglas. I nodded at Darius and Doreen as I walked out of 5a, not giving them chance to repeat their emotional farewell from the last time I'd left.

I unlocked the Shed of Necessity, pushed the scooter out, and wheeled it down the alley to the front of 5a. The scooter started with the first turn of the key. I didn't want to be on the roads. I didn't want to get to where the roads would lead me. Most importantly, I didn't want anyone else to die.

I revved the engine and realised suddenly that I couldn't remember Thoughtless's voice. It felt like a let-go and an add-on both at the same time. It felt like a double punishment.

I figured I deserved it.

12.

I managed the scooter better than I had expected. I didn't come close to falling off. The power of intention is amazing.

I parked and ran towards Morgan's front door.

It was unlocked. That was not what I wanted.

I forced myself to rush inside.

Barry was in the lounge. He was on his knees. His nose looked broken, his eyes were swollen, and his lips were bloody.

I reached down and helped him to his feet.

'What happened?'

'I...I was here and he came for her.' Barry struggled to speak.

'Who came for her?'

205

'Thad...Thaddeus. He was raging. I told her not to let him in.' Barry slumped and I caught him. He looked at me in a way I couldn't have imagined just a few hours earlier. 'It was like he thought she was his property, like he owned her. He said he couldn't let her leave him. He said he'd given her a chance to change her mind, and she hadn't taken it.'

I held Barry against me. 'What happened next?'

'He went to grab her, to hit her and take her away. I charged at him. I was only here because I knew how Morgan secretly felt about you, and I wanted to tell her that you could be trusted, that, after what happened in the park, I knew you were good for her.'

'And then?'

'I couldn't stop him.' Barry sobbed. 'He was so ferocious. He knocked me down and took her. I'm so sorry.' He fell against my chest. I felt his heart, pumping as if it was going to burst.

'Do you know where he was taking her?'

'Back to his home. Back to the Garden Centre. You need to get there fast as you can.'

'I'll ring for an ambulance for you, first.'

'I can look after myself.' Barry pushed himself away from me. 'You go and look after Morgan. Go! Now!'

He was right. I could hear Bella telling me that he was. I turned for the door.

'Jack, one other thing!' Barry reached a hand onto my shoulder. I looked back. 'He said he was going to give her a hen party she would never forget.'

I sprinted back to the scooter.

13.

The Mad Geranium Garden Centre was a couple of

miles out of town. It was the place where Morgan had taught me how to create my garden. She had worked there until she had ended her relationship with Thaddeus.

The Mad Geranium had been established by Thad's father. His son had taken over the reins several years ago. It was a popular place.

But not at this time of night.

The roads were deserted.

I got there fast and safe.

I pulled into the car park. The lights were on in the shop. I could see Thad and Morgan standing, facing each other. He had his left hand round her throat. He was holding what looked like a bottle of champagne in his right.

Behind Morgan, three women were tied into chairs. They were all gagged. They all looked terrified. I didn't recognise any of them.

I felt sick.

Morgan saw me as I walked towards the large, glass sliding doors. Thad saw me, too. His surprise turned into something very different, very quickly. It turned into something cold. Something I'd never seen before.

I had no choice but to keep walking.

Thaddeus moved behind the counter, forcing Morgan with him. He pressed a button. The doors opened. I stepped inside. Thaddeus marched Morgan back to their original position. I could see now just how tightly he was gripping her throat. She seemed barely conscious. I couldn't tell if that was due to fear, lack of oxygen, or both.

I heard the doors close.

The woman in the chair nearest to me tried to scream something at me, despite the tape over her mouth.

I forced myself to ignore her.

Thaddeus and I stared at each other.

He spoke first.

'What are you doing here, Jack?'

'I came to save Morgan from a madman.' My voice was suddenly fluid and strong, as if the breath that was carrying it was coming from somewhere other than me.

'What makes you think he's a madman?' Thad's nostrils flared. 'What makes you the expert?'

'You don't have to be an expert to know that only a psycho-nut-job could do the things this guy has done.'

'Is that what you think? That he's a psycho?'

'What would you call him?'

'It doesn't matter what I'd call him. Other people should call him a Lord.'

'If you have the power of a Lord, why don't you let Morgan go?'

Thaddeus growled. His right palm lashed out without warning, catching Morgan flush on the side of her face. It landed with a sickly, heavy, wet sound. She collapsed unconscious at his feet. He didn't watch her fall. He kept his eyes on me as he reached behind him, grabbed one of the chairs from near the counter, and skidded it across the floor towards me. 'Sit down.'

'What if I don't?'

'I'll stamp on her head.'

I sat.

'I'm going to ask you some questions,' he said. 'You're going to answer quickly and honestly. Any time you fail to do that, I'm going to stamp on her head. Do you understand?'

'Yes.'

'Good. Keep very still.' He half-turned away as he reached towards the light-control panel. He switched all the lights off, apart from one directly above me. 'That's better. Now you're in the spotlight, we'll begin.'

'Who knows you're here?'

'No one.'

'How did you know it was me?'

'Barry sounded the alarm. He told me because he knew I'd been out on patrol.'

'What?'

'I'd seen a thing in the news about...about when you started out. Although it was a minor story, I took it upon myself to go out every night, keeping watch.'

'Alone?'

'Yes.'

'You didn't do so well.'

'No.'

'What did you do about tonight's little foray?'

'I called the police, told them...told them...about the crime scene. I didn't give them my name or number.'

'Why not?'

'I don't want to get involved with the police.'

'That would have been better than getting involved with me.'

'Yes.'

Thaddeus looked at Morgan, unmoving on the floor. He looked at the other women.

'I gave her the chance to accept that she'd made a mistake by breaking off our engagement. That was my error. She thought it meant I would let her go. I never will. After I've finished with you, we'll get back to her hen party. I got these three as special guests. They're working girls. I'm going to show Morgan just who I am. I'm going to show her what I do to women like these. Then she will understand fully why she can never leave.'

Thaddeus paused, scratched his nose, took a long swig

of champagne.

'Have you ever been married?' He asked.

'No.'

'Long-term girlfriend?'

'No.'

'You don't know what it's like, then?'

'No.'

'You don't know what you have the right to expect?'

'No.'

'I'll tell you.' He stepped towards me. 'You have the right to be recognised, that's first and foremost. You have the right to be understood.

'There shouldn't be any secrets between the two of you, because they know you for who you really are. And they should be grateful because you're special. You wouldn't want to marry someone if they weren't special, would you? But you can't know that someone's special unless you really understand them in the first place! Can you?'

'I guess not.'

'Exactly.' He pointed back at Morgan. 'I wanted her to recognise who I was! I thought, if she truly loves me, she'll see the real me and understand it. All I wanted from her was to be seen and felt! Is that too much to ask?'

'No.'

'Exactly! But she couldn't do it. She's so blinded by what people call love, and by all the shit that goes with it, that she has no idea who I really am! She doesn't even want to know! Do you understand how tragic that is?'

'I'm trying to.'

'The truth is, women aren't interested in men. They don't really want to get to know us, to understand what we really need. No, they're just after the fantasy of love. Whatever that means. And the ones who aren't after that fantasy – the women like these three here - ' he gestured with the bottle towards the prostitutes, ' – they're already dead. They stopped feeling things years ago. Do you see?'

I closed my eyes.

'See?'

'Yes.'

'These women – these prostitutes – they don't even notice the men who have sex them. They're a million miles away, doing their own thing in their own minds, when they should be giving men their attention. Did you know that?'

'No.'

'Have you ever paid for a whore?'

'No.'

'Save your money. You won't ever get their attention. Are you listening?'

'Yes.'

I opened my eyes.

He was watching me, rubbing his chin with the thumb and forefinger of his left hand.

'So, you really told no one you were coming here?'

'No.'

'So you were in luck, and out of luck, at the same time,' he said. 'And now your situation is hopeless.'

'I guess so.'

'No guesswork needed.' He pointed at Morgan again, then switched his focus back onto me. 'She's got a new life ahead of her. You, though, you haven't got much life left at all.'

I risked a question, hoping that Morgan might at least regain consciousness and make a break for it.

'When did you decide to be so...special?'

He considered briefly. He closed the distance between us as he spoke.

'My father taught me that you must always aim high. He started out with nothing. He knew nothing. He owned nothing. But he learnt who he secretly was and built this business. He always used to tell me that every boy could grow up and create their own power, they could be in control of as many people as they chose. *Lad then lord*, that was his motto. *Lad then lord*, from nothing to something, from no one to someone. That's what inspired me.'

The single light above me shimmered suddenly. I wondered if the electricity was about to fail.

Thaddeus appeared not to notice.

I pushed another question. 'How are you going to kill me?'

He shrugged as he came another step closer. The light shimmered a second time. 'Are you going to fight?'

'No.'

'Why not?'

'I don't know how to.'

He shrugged again. 'I won't enjoy it.'

'Because I won't fight back?'

'Because you're a bloke.'

'What difference does that make?'

'Enough talking,' he said, reaching into his jacket pocket and pulled out a knife. 'It's time.'

Thaddeus raised the blade. The light shimmered again. He still paid it no attention. He lunged forwards, aiming for my face.

Ricky's sidekick caught him flush on his knee. Thaddeus's charge stopped dead. He buckled. Ricky swept his feet from under him. He fell face down. He was unconscious before he hit the floor. It was only the second time in my life I had seen a Shade make physical contact with a person, and it was over in an instant.

'Ricky!' I leaped to my feet, arms outstretched, reaching for my dead brother. He disappeared so quickly I didn't even see him go.

I did see Morgan, upright on the floor, staring at me with her mouth open.

15.

The next thirty-six hours were filled with interviews, explanations, half-truths and lies. There were hugs and tears, sceptical cold-eyed challenges, warnings, calm reassurances, cross-checks, expressions of grudging acceptance and shows of gratitude. There was disbelief and relief in almost equal measure.

It felt like no-man's land.

Eventually, though, we all made it across safely.

Morgan told the police that she would have died without my help. Barry told them how Thaddeus had kidnapped her. I don't know exactly what the three prostitutes said.

Bean, Stew, Wee Drop and The Paddington Fish all told their own stories. They had enough in common, laced with some inevitable variation, to be accepted as factual. The body of Thoughtless spoke silent, irresistible truth.

I claimed that my karate skills must have come from watching my brother practise, and helping him train, all those years ago.

The questions stopped when photos of the murdered girls were found in a safe hidden in Thaddeus's office. He'd kept a record of his kills. He'd got close-ups of his violence.

There were seven victims in all. The first four were working girls from the other side of the city. The final three were my friends.

The Beginning

Anne-Marie Rose Fairbank

1.

I'd never known Thoughtless's real name. I'd never asked her. There hadn't seemed any benefit in knowing. She was – she had been - Thoughtless, in the best possible of ways.

I discovered that she had been christened Anne-Marie Rose Fairbank when her parents asked me to be the Celebrant at her funeral.

It helped having a different, almost foreign, name to refer to her by. It helped me manage my emotions - until the very end of the ceremony, until the moment when her Shade stepped through the door I couldn't see.

Until then, I'd presumed that, as her Shade was present, Thoughtless would be coming home with me.

My presumption existed because I'd never seen a Shade move on before. I was simply expecting more of what I already knew. It's an easy mistake to make.

Another, even more significant, presumption was also just about to be shattered.

It happened outside the crematorium. Morgan was standing by my side, as we watched Thoughtless's family members trying to find some common ground with Bean, Stew and Barry.

'I saw her, too.' Morgan said, looking straight ahead.

'You saw who?'[26]

'Thoughtless's Shade.' She kept her eyes fixed on the

---

[26] I know I should have said, 'whom?', but it's difficult to be linguistically correct when the woman you are crazy about suddenly implies something you'd never thought possible.

group of mourners.

'How?'

'With my eyes.' A dry smile creased her face. 'They changed when Thaddeus knocked me out, and I banged my head on the floor.'

'How...How do you know they changed then?'

'Because I saw Ricky save you. I saw him kick Thaddeus.'

'You saw that?'

'Yes. I recognised Ricky from those photos you showed me years ago.'

'Why didn't you say something before?'

'When exactly? It's been busy and challenging of late.'

'True.'

'Are you going to be able to cope?'

'Cope with what?'

'Not being the only psychic medium in The Frog & Bull.'

'Given that it's you, I'm sure I'll learn to.'

She squeezed my hand, and a brand-new life experience revealed itself.

'I'll be able to introduce you to Bella!'

'And Doreen and Darius.'

'Yes. Yes, of course. It's just that - '

'- Bella is family.'

'Yes.'

'That was obvious from the moment you first told me about her.'

It was my turn to squeeze Morgan's hand. 'It seems we've got even more to talk about than I thought.'

'We can make a start later tonight, after your gig.' This time her smile was triumphant.

'Unless you have to spend all of your time consoling me.'

'You'll be great.'

'I hope so. Before then, me and boys are having a chat. Our first real one since...since it all happened.'

'I'm sure you will all look after each other. That's what you do in your own, unique ways.'

'Yeah. We'll get there – wherever there is – eventually.'

'Thoughtless wouldn't want anything else.'

'I know.'

2.

When Bean, Stew and I met in The Frog & Bull later that afternoon, we didn't know quite where, or how, to begin.

I started the ball rolling.

'Any chance the other two are coming?'

Bean shook his head. 'No. The Fish told me he needed to get underwater, and Wee Drop's disappeared again.'

'But he can't walk!'

'Maybe somebody picked him up.'

'Yeah.'

'Maybe he's got family.'

'Yeah.'

I looked at Stew, willing him to give the conversation-ball some momentum.

'Have you got a headache?' He asked.

'No. Why?'

'You look like you might have, that's all.'

We fell silent again.

Barry brought over our first round of free drinks. He thudded them down, spilt liquid from each glass, and returned to the bar without saying a word.

Bean sighed again.

The ball clearly wasn't going to roll quickly unless I

hoofed it as hard as I possibly could.

'We have to talk about stuff,' I said. 'Get back to something like normal as quickly as possible.'

'Please don't say we're going to have our own new normal.' Bean shifted in his seat. 'I've had enough new normals in the last couple of years to last a lifetime.'

'You've adjusted well to each one,' I said.

'D'you reckon?'

'Absolutely,' I realised I'd never told him before. 'I wouldn't have coped as well as you if I'd had a leg removed. And I definitely wouldn't be able to Boom-Ka-Ka-Chow with a prosthetic.'

'Pain wears you down,' Bean said. 'You reach a point when you'll accept anything to get rid of it. Plus, you can hardly complain when it's your own fault.'

'We all make mistakes.'

'A mistake is a thing you get wrong once and then learn from. I didn't make a mistake. I'm a diabetic who can't stop drinking; who's never going to try to stop drinking. That's called deciding your own fate.' Bean tapped his left thigh. 'At least this mix of thermoplastics, silicone, titanium and other stuff can't be damaged by my drinking decisions.'

'Are you sure it's worth it?'

'I'm sure it's better than the alternative. And I am choosing how I go.'

We all fell silent again.

Stew raised his glass. 'To Thoughtless,' he said. 'To Thoughtless and the others who never got to choose.'

We all drank long and hard.

'And I've got something new to look forward to,' Bean said.

'What's that?' Stew asked.

'Accommodation when I die. I'm going to move into 5a

218

and haunt Jack.'

'You'll be welcome,' I said. 'Only it wouldn't matter whether you were welcome or not. I can't keep you out. Doors and windows don't work against Shades. Oh, and by the way, you won't be haunting me. Not really. Not technically. You'll be more like my housemate than anything else. Anyway, we've got years before we need to consider that.'

I drained my glass. The other two followed suit. I signalled to Barry for another round. He waved in response.

Stew leant forwards. 'You did a great job unlocking dat droll hen,' he said to me, before tapping Bean on his shoulder. 'We should have worked that out straight away.'

'I don't see why,' I said. 'You don't know Morgan like I do. It was a clue that was best suited to me, just like some questions are best suited to one of you.'

'He's right,' Bean said. 'We complement each other, that's what makes us such a good team.'

'You're right,' I said. 'We do.'

'Even though we hardly ever actually compliment each other,' Stew said.

'Then maybe we should start?' I suggested.

'That would make it a new normal,' Bean said. 'And we just agreed that wasn't in our future.'

Our beers arrived.

Bean led the toast. 'To avoiding the new normal.'

We echoed the sentiment.

'There was something else about dat droll hen,' I said. 'It came to me when I was at The Mad Geranium, before the boys in blue burst on to the scene.'

'What is it?'

'Dat droll hen really is an anagram, after all.'

'You're kidding?'

'Nope.'

'You're genuinely not just winding us up?'

'Nope.'

Bean and Stew shifted automatically into their quizzing postures.

'Just give us a minute,' Bean said.

'Your time starts now,' I said.

Stew got there first, pressing the imaginary buzzer just a fraction of a second ahead of Bean.

'Mr Gardner, what have you got for me?'

Stew was wide-eyed. 'How incredible is this?'

'I'm afraid that's the wrong answer.'

'No, I mean, it's incredible. You're right. It was the perfect clue. Dat droll hen is *Thad Loldren*.'

'Correct.'

'And, ironically,' Bean added, keen to prove that he was also up-to-speed, 'Thaddeus, which is the complete version of his name, coming from the Greek Thaddaios, means courageous heart. He couldn't have been named more wrongly.'

'That will have been his dad's doing,' I said. 'I think he was a control freak. He played his part in dat droll hen, too.'

'How so?' Bean's head jerked back.

'There's a fourth interpretation.'

'No way!'

'Way.'

'Go on, then.'

'The dad's motto, the one he instilled into his son was, *lad then lord*. It was meant to be a motivational rags-to-riches philosophy, but Thad interpreted it very differently. Anyway, *lad then lord* -'

'- Is dat droll hen', Bean finished it for me.

'Wow!' Stew sat back and looked up at the ceiling. 'We

had the past, present and future all in one conundrum.'

'It's like the black hole of anagrams,' Bean said.

'Good job we weren't drawn in and destroyed,' I said.

'It obviously wasn't our time,' Bean said.

We drank a third toast, in silence. I sensed that we were all wondering when it would be our time.

'Do you think it was his dad's influence that turned Thad into a killer?' Stew asked.

'I don't know,' I said. 'I think it's a mixed-up mess.' I had another drink. I felt my heart force out some honest sounds. My eyes watered as I spoke. 'I just wish there wasn't such horror in our world. I just wish people didn't...' My voice trailed off as my mind filled with an image of Thaddeus approaching me with his knife in hand.

Bean offered me a way out. 'Time for some puns about change!' He winked at me, making sure Stew couldn't see. 'Let's get you warmed up for tonight's performance.'

I clapped my hands, partly as a sign of acceptance and partly in gratitude. This wasn't a new normal. This was how we used to be.

I started punning immediately.

'There was a time when I wanted to be Velcro, so I could just pull myself together.'

'And?'

'I tried to be shoe leather, but I didn't take a shine to it.'

'And?'

'Once I thought I was a set of press studs, but I managed to snap out of it.'

'And?'

'Oh, come on! Give me a break!'

Bean was having none of it. 'One more.'

'Ok. I used to believe I was a cashmere sweater, but I was just pulling the wool over my eyes.'

Bean and Stew broke into spontaneous applause.

I bowed cautiously, waiting for the sting in the tail. Today there wasn't one.

'Welcome back to all of us,' Bean said.

'Couldn't agree more,' Stew said. 'It suddenly feels like we're back where we started.'

'It does, indeed,' Bean said. 'So now I'm going to the Gents and when I come back -'

'- Sad Puddings!' Stew said. 'We'll have a special round, just for Jack.'

3.

It was called Commentary. It was a single player game. And the single player who only ever played it, was me. As the Master of the Cards, Stew chose two cards at random. The first identified the topic that had to be addressed, the second revealed the commentary style in which it had to be done.

Today, Stew came up with 'The State of the World' delivered in the style of a horse racing commentator.

I drank some beer and cleared my throat, ready to deliver a quick-fire monologue in my best horse racing commentator's voice.[27]

Stew cued me in with a silent five-four-three-two-one countdown, and I was off – if you'll pardon the pun - leaning forward slightly and talking into my hand as if it were a microphone.

'And we're in the final furlong of the Everything To Play For Stakes and it's turned into a two-horse race between Fascism and Global Warming. It's Fascism, lying in second place. It's been lying throughout the race, but it's

---

[27] Again, it's as bad as my Kevin McCloud impression.

lying very well in second now.

'It's Fascism and Global Warming. Fascism, out of Divide And Conquer, by They'll Fall For It This Time, in the black and brown. Global Warming, out of Control by Who Cares About The Future, in the bright yellow.

'They're into the final stretch and Global Warming is picking up pace. Things are really heating up, but Fascism is coming up strong on the far right. Fascism using the whip. It's Fascism, and Global Warming, it's between these two. Coming to the line, it's Fascism, Global Warming, Fascism, Global Warming - and it's Fascism who gets there, just ahead of Global Warming! Fascism saluting in triumph as Global Warming comes in second - and just keeps on going!

'The result is in, but, for Global Warming, the race isn't over! The race isn't over! Oh, it is now! The human race is over! Fascism wiped out, along with everything else! Apart from the spiders, the insects and the rats, the spiders, the insects and the rats. They're in charge now, and it all starts again here in the Everything To Play For Stakes! Back to you in the universal studio.'

I lowered my microphone-hand, sat back in my chair, and drained my glass.

Bean and Stew nodded in appreciation.

'I fear that makes me smile because it's tragically true, and humour is the only available escape route,' Bean said.

'There is a glimmer of hope, if you remember that a horse race is ultimately linear and that we actually live in a spiral universe,' Stew reminded us.

'The problem with the notion of a spiral,' Bean said, 'is that implies that things will keep returning. And that is what we are seeing, things returning in the worst of ways.'

'It implies that good things will keep returning, too,' Stew countered.

'It does feel, though, that some attitudes haven't changed and that some very unwanted behaviours are becoming more common place.' Bean addressed me. 'I know it's different for me and Stew,' he said. 'We're white men in what is still regarded by too many as an essentially white nation. That means, however much we try, we can't imagine what it's been like - still is like – for you. Frankly, I'd sooner be a one-legged, drunken white diabetic, than a man of colour like yourself.'

'And Windrush was a disgrace,' Stew said.

I folded my beer mat in half. 'At least my parents missed it,' I said. 'They didn't deserve to die when they did, but at least they missed that. They believed in this country. If they'd been threatened with deportation, it would have been the worst thing ever.'

'To small graces,' Stew said.

We raised our glasses for a fourth time.

'To small graces,' I said.

We looked at each other in silence as we drank.

4.

I stayed in the pub until my gig was due to start. Barry let me change in an upstairs room. Morgan had organised an audience. She joined Bean and Stew at our usual table. Barry watched from behind the bar.

I had only new material. There was no safety net. But then, the only thing that could fall was my ego, and I had the strange sense that it was more elastic than I'd ever realised.

'Just go with the flow,' I silently told myself. 'And if you trip up, just roll.' An image of Thoughtless stretched briefly behind my eyes.

I looked at Morgan and nodded. Then I let my mouth

get on with it.

'When I worked as an estate agent, I tried selling a building made entirely out of bran. I told the client it was a barn conversion.

'Then I ran a successful concussion clinic – absolute knockout.

'Then I had a great construction business – built that from the ground up.

'Then I created a business selling cures for eczema – started from scratch.

'When I won the title of the World's Best Thief, I had to pinch myself. Which, ironically, is what I did to win the title.

'Competition was fierce. I beat the Laundrette Robbers, they always made a clean getaway. I beat the Stocking Gang, they were responsible for a number of hold-ups before being put away for a long stretch. And the Barber's Boys, a trio who stole only from Gents Hairdressers. What do I think of the jury's decision to find them guilty? It was cut and dry.

'I do come from a criminal family. My uncle, Peter, was known in the underworld as Peter Ding Dong Jones. Does that name ring a bell?

'He was arrested once for stealing one hundred and fifty bundles of straw. He was released on bail.

'Hay!

'That's the best pun I've ever written – according to a straw poll.

'From now on, all of my humour is on the wain...'

The audience were on my side every step of the way. I ended up doing more than I had planned. The atmosphere in The Frog & Bull was better than I had ever experienced. And Morgan was with me throughout.

It was 11pm, the adrenaline was beginning to wear off,

when Barry took me to one side and delivered the news that I couldn't have expected.

'The DCI in charge of the Thaddeus case gave a press conference earlier. It turns out that the DNA found at Thoughtless's crime scene is different to the others. It doesn't belong to Thaddeus. That means he had an accomplice. There's a partner, another killer, who's still out there.'

'Oh, dear God!'

'Absolutely.'

'And Thaddeus?'

'From what I understand, he's making it clear that he knows who it is, but he's saying nothing more.'

'That's how he knew that Thoughtless had been killed; his partner had already told him.'

'Yeah.'

'When he referred to that night's *foray*, in his mocking, arrogant way, I presumed he'd done it himself.'

'He wanted you to.'

'What a bastard.'

I walked outside. I left the noise of the pub behind. I stood on the street and looked up at Infinity. It seemed unmoved.

Morgan was suddenly by my side. My hand was suddenly in hers. She didn't speak for at least a minute.

Then she said, 'We've got to catch him. Together. The Shades will help us. And now that I can communicate with them, too, we are twice the force we were. You didn't leave Bella's murder unpunished, so we can't let Thoughtless's killer get away with it.'

She was right. It was the very last thing I wanted, the very last I would have ever considered, but I couldn't live with myself if I stopped now. And, this time, I'd have a very different partner helping me. 'It's not just for Thoughtless,'

I said. 'It's for the girls that will be killed if we don't stop him.'

'Let's drink to that,' Morgan said. 'And let's start tomorrow.'

'How?'

'We'll give ourselves a name. Just something between us, something that might help soften the edges.'

'Like what?'

'We'll call ourselves...' The smile came before the words. '...The Shades Detective Agency.'

'Very droll.'

'Is it a deal?'

'Yes, it's the most important deal.'

'I think so, too.'

We kissed. It was amazing. Then we went inside and did our best to get drunk.

5.

I sobered up as soon as I walked into 5a.

The Shades were standing in the lounge. Darius and Doreen were watching Bella. She was completely still, yet she was dominating the room. I'd never seen, or felt, such stillness.

I was drawn towards her. I managed only one step before an invisible something barred my way.

Bella looked at me and smiled. I can't begin to tell you the different notes that played in that smile. Her beautiful light-blues shone with a brightness I didn't recognise. Her edges shimmered.

'It's here, Jack,' she said. 'The door's here.'

She gestured to her right.

'It's not the door we tried to open and couldn't. It's the door that opens to somewhere else.'

A heavy, ice-cold hand gripped my chest.

'I thought you wanted to stay here forever?'

'I did. I really did. That feeling is still there, sort of. It's just so far away now and it's changed. It's softened. It's comfortable. It's not spiking me anymore.' Her smile returned and played its music. 'I let go of something and the door appeared. Do you understand?'

My nose fizzed. My eyes watered.

'Yes.'

'I knew you would.'

'When are you going?'

'Now.'

'Couldn't you, maybe, wait until the morning?'

'No, Jack. The door's open now.' The smile softened, saddened, swelled gradually.

I couldn't change the tune. I knew that. That's why I was so scared.

'I'm taking Doreen and Darius,' she said. 'They can't see the door, but they trust me, and we need to stay together. For this part, at least.'

Bella shimmered some more. Or maybe my tears were just blurring my vision. Or maybe it was both.

'I had to wait to say goodbye,' she said. 'But I can't hold this any longer. I love you, Jack.'

Doreen stepped forwards. She looked at me, whispered, 'Thank you,' and stepped to Bella's right.

'Maybe Eliot is somewhere through that door,' Darius said. 'If Epiah Khan is, I'll give him your...' His voice gave way as he choked back a sob. He looked down at his feet as he joined the other two.

Only Bella was beyond the emotion of it all.

I think she blew me a kiss, but I couldn't be sure. I think she whispered something gently to the other two.

Then she stepped forwards without hesitation and the

three of them disappeared.

It happened so swiftly it threatened to tear my mind apart, to rip out the very foundation of everything. The Black Hole swirled and pulled. My head began spinning. The Black Hole roared. I had no reason to fight it. I let myself go. I fell to the floor.

Bella's voice cut through the noise.

'Oh my God!' She was laughing uncontrollably, like I'd never heard her before. She was laughing so much she was struggling to get the words out. 'Oh my God!' She laughed again.

The Black Hole disappeared, blown over the horizon by her energy from that other place. Suddenly, I was on solid ground. I slapped the carpet with my hand.

'What's it like?' I shouted after her. 'What can you see?'

Her laughter filled the room.

'I've no idea!' She squealed.

And then she was gone.

6.

I fell asleep on the floor.

When I woke up, the morning was opening its eyes, too. I went out into the garden to greet it.

Two Protective Pigeons fluttered down onto the Shed of Necessity. I felt like they knew they'd missed something. I told them there were somethings they couldn't protect me from. From the way they looked at each and nodded, I think they already knew that.

I walked over to the Lavvies, ran my hands through them, and thanked them silently for their scent.

Clouds scurried overhead.

'Everyone goes,' I said to the Settled-in-Sparrows. 'Sooner or later we all leave.'

It was impossible not to wonder where Bella was right now. I'd have given anything to know how she'd changed. To see what else she had lost and, more importantly, what that loss revealed. I guessed if I met her again, I'd love her more than I ever had.

I caught a movement out of the corner of my eyes. The Synchronised Squirrels were running along the walls. One had something in its mouth. The other looked just a little bit embarrassed. I hadn't seen them for a couple of days. It was good to know they were Ok.

My garden is as much a memorial to my parents, as it is a sanctuary for me. They'd both been keen gardeners. I used to think they were crazy for spending so much of their free time looking after plants. It's funny how wrong we can be.

I smelled the Lavvies again.

I don't know how much of everything we can ever really work out. I finally got somewhere useful with dat droll hen, but it took too long. And it still might not have been everything there was.

Barry, the landlord, was dat droll hen.

Morgan, the woman I believe is my forever partner, was dat droll hen.

Thad Loldren, the p-n-j was dat droll hen.

Lad then lord, the father's motivation that Thad had adopted, was dat droll hen.

Four levels of truth. All interconnected. Each one a doorway to the next. Each one presenting challenges, the likelihood of loss, realisations that took something away from my life or added something amazing into it – or did both simultaneously. And neither the taking away nor the adding-on was painless, even if it was valuable.

I got to four levels of truth.

There were probably more.

There usually is.

Life's complex.

No wonder people prefer headlines.

7.

A day passed before the final headline came in.

It came, as all headlines do, in a variety of guises. Each one, though, carried the same message:

Thaddeus Loldren had beaten the system.

He had found a way to escape the punishment he deserved.

Somehow, he had managed to get hold of a length of material. It was just enough to set him free.

He hung himself in the privacy of his cell.

It was some time before a prison warder found the body. He called immediately for medical help and did everything in his power to restart the heart. He failed.

Thaddeus Loldren was pronounced dead at 9.05pm.

Thaddeus

1.

He moved in with me less than three hours later.

'The Universe wounds us
so that it can enter more easily.'
Epiah Khan

Printed in Poland
by Amazon Fulfillment
Poland Sp. z o.o., Wrocław
19 August 2023

710fb6a9-5c0d-4e5a-b39c-e1367287d037R01